John Cooper Presents

The Great Reveal

Ex-Scotland Yard Detective Exposes Child Trafficking & Satanic Ritual Abuse

With Guest

Jon Wedger

YouTube.com/TheJohnCooperShow

thejohncoopershow@gmail.com

First Printing – 2023

1 North Rd, N7 9HD,
London, United Kingdom

CONTENTS

Foreword

When it comes to truth-seeking and unwavering dedication to justice, there exists a rare breed of individuals who rise above the shadows, propelled by an unyielding commitment to protect the innocent.

Jon Wedger, a former police detective and now whistle blower, embodies this courageous spirit. With resolute determination, and sense of duty, he embarked on a path that would unravel the darkest secrets lurking within our society.

This book, aptly titled The Great Reveal, delves into a gripping three-part interview series that reveals a heart-wrenching truth about innocent children's experiences, bringing to light a horrifying world of exploitation, unspeakable acts of paedophilia and ritualistic murder, that has been buried and hidden from sight... until now.

The first episode thrusts us into the depths of Jon's career within the Met Police; into the seedy underbelly of society which soon led him to a startling realisation: paedophilia permeates far beyond the grimy streets, stretching its vile tentacles up to senior officers within the police, government officials, and even royalty.

Instead of being applauded and commemorated for his valiant efforts in uncovering this evil network, Jon found himself dragged into an office, where he was given an ultimatum; stand down and keep silent or face the unleashed fury of a system determined to crush him.

In the second episode, we bear witness to the harrowing discoveries that awaited Jon as he peered deeper into the abyss, unveiling an insidious satanic ritual hierarchy where innocent children or "diamonds" are ruthlessly abducted and subjected to unimaginable horrors – bound, tortured, and ultimately sacrificed in grotesque acts of depravity. Their blood is spilled, their screams silenced, all in the name of devotion to demonic entities.

In the final episode of this series, the focus shifts to the power of mind control. Jon exposes the mechanisms employed to shatter the minds of these innocent souls, fracturing their identities through trauma and manipulation. The consequences reverberate throughout society, infiltrating the world of Hollywood, the music and entertainment industry and beyond, where mind-controlled individuals become mere pawns in a larger game of societal control.

Jon Wedger's journey stands as a testament to unwavering resolve, despite facing threats and attempts to dismantle his life. He stood firm in the face of immense pressure and bullying, peeling back the layers of secrecy to expose the stark reality of the world we live in.

Editor's Notes

In order to bring Jon's powerful narrative to light, I recorded three in-depth interviews with him, for my podcast Raising the Bar, capturing his words and experiences in their rawest form. Throughout the transcription process, I have strived to preserve the authenticity and live conversational feel, keeping his colloquial speech intact while tidying up the occasional sentence for clarity and ensure a smooth reading experience.

To provide a more comprehensive understanding, I have included excerpts from a bonus interview I did with Jon for my Patreon members, carefully transcribed and seamlessly woven into the narrative. These additional insights serve to fill the missing gaps and offer a complete picture of Jon's journey.

I must also address the topic of satanic ritual abuse, which features prominently in Jon's account. Whilst I acknowledge that not everyone shares religious beliefs, it is important to recognise that there are individuals who genuinely adhere to satanic practices and worship dark forces. This book aims to shed light on their activities and the profound impact they have on innocent lives. Please approach these sections with an open mind, understanding that they reflect the experiences and perceptions of those involved, not necessarily our own beliefs.

Lastly, I'd really appreciate it if you could leave a review of this book as it helps in the Amazon searches. Also please share this book with your friends, especially those who may be unaware of the hidden truths that pervade our society. By raising awareness and initiating conversations, we can collectively work towards exposing the darkness that lurks beneath the surface and ultimately bring about positive change.

So, dear reader, fasten your seatbelt, for we are about to embark on a spirited expedition into the dark unknown. With every turn of the page, we inch closer to the truths that have long been concealed.

This is not just Jon's story — this is a collective awakening.

The Great Reveal - John Cooper
Interviewer/Editor; Raising the Bar (The John Cooper Show)

Part 1 - Exposing Paedophilia in Government

Cooper: Hi, everyone, welcome to another episode of Raising the Bar with myself John Cooper, and today, I'm very grateful to have on the show, Jon Wedger.

Jon is a former Scotland Yard detective that spent 25 years in the force and is now an author and whistle blower who campaigns to expose an establishment cover-up of child abuse. Jon has travelled around the UK and Europe talking to victims and survivors of child abuse and whistle blowers from a wide range of professional industries. Working hard to put pressure on the government and mainstream media to hold power to account and put children first.

Jon, welcome to the show mate.

Wedger: Pleasure, John.

Cooper: No, I'm really grateful to have you on buddy, really am.

We've got a lot to talk about, haven't we? A lot to talk about. I mean… I've been following your work for quite a while now and I know it's brilliant work and I know that you've gone through… well, to hell and back really, from what I've read about you and seen from you.

Wedger: On many levels, on many levels.

Cooper: On many levels. So, what I was thinking was, could we go into your past? You worked as a detective in the Metropolitan Police. Could we talk a little bit about that and the culture in the police? What it was like in the 90's, 80's, however far back it went and then we move into the cover-ups that were going on, the paedophilia, the child abuse, the child trafficking, that is still rife today, right?

Wedger: Yeah, and I think if anything, it's getting worse.

Cooper: Is it really?

Wedger: It's strange because when I joined the police it was very structured but now it's in disarray and they've got rid of what they call "the old sweats", the old school detectives and coppers.

We had a tradecraft, and it was a skill and they took a lot of effort in training you but now they're just short of people. A lot of the experienced ones have retired, some have left, and they're just pushing people through so quick. The public are always commenting on the difference and there *is* a difference. You can tell by the uniform, there's a difference.

The "bobby on the beat" isn't anymore. It's very paramilitary. You see with a lot of these podcasts that are going out, you know the sort of little Facebook posts that people are putting out, when they have interactions with the police, the police are so robotic and you're seeing it in America, Canada. We're seeing the same attitude going on and they've become corporatists, they really have.

Cooper: They're "policy" officers. Not really people of the streets; public servants anymore, right?

Wedger: And some of them are coming across as very thick you know.

You see them with their fingers in [their vest] and I'm not denigrating them because they were my brothers and sisters and I think I'm proud to serve in the police. At the same time, the police have hurt me monumentally. They've damaged me. I'm not anti-police, I'm anti-corruption and when you have corruption, you have a virus, you have a fungus, you have a disease that just sweeps through everything. You have corruption however in the police. We have corruption in high office, it *is* in high office.

Cooper: And it's getting worse, would you say?

Wedger: Yeah, because people aren't challenging it and it's really odd. I mean, I'll go through the timeline of my career in a minute but I will tell you one thing, my journey has taken me in and out of parliament many, many times. I've been before the great and the good of British politics.

I was meant to meet up with the Home Secretary a couple of months ago but due to all this whatever we've got going on in this country [Covid], that's been put on hold.

Theresa May mentioned me once at a parliamentary meeting when she was PM and I went before a policing and crime minister and then I went before my constituent MP, who was a former police and crime minister and there were representatives from... I forgot who the Home Secretary at the time was, I really can't remember but she sent down her second in charge and it was to do with my role as a whistle blower and speaking out.

This politician turned around to me and said, "Jon, hopefully this will stop now because there are rules, there is legislation, there are guidelines, there are protocols now, that whistle blowers aren't bullied".

I said, "yeah, and there are laws saying you shouldn't have sex with children but you know what, quelle surprise, people still do".

And this is a level of naivety on their part you know. They all say you shouldn't speed but everyone does. It's just a nonsense.

Unless these things are managed and policed properly, they're futile, they're pointless and this is what happens. What I found was that the cover-ups went very much to the heart of the establishment. I was then later, not only to expose child abuse, but it then lead onto organised criminality.

I spent a lot of time in the last few years working with ex-very serious and organised criminals. Some of them have got massive notoriety, not just in the UK but globally and they're working very closely with me and it has taken me all over the place but then I started also dealing with a thing called "satanic ritual abuse" (SRA) and this is where it gets dirty and this is where you start seeing cover-ups and the need for a cover-up. So, I'd like to spend a bit of time if I may John, going into that and how it manifests and how it hides and how it manipulates and bullies society generally.

Cooper: Absolutely and the thing is, if you start to talk about it, you'll immediately get your character assassinated and people start calling you labels and say, "oh, this is conspiracy theory", to try and bury it, I guess. Because there are so many accounts of this now, it's getting to the point where you can't hide this anymore.

Wedger: No, and I like to go on about victimology - why victims behave the way they do, why people behave the way they do and so many people of different levels of healing have come to me.

Some are resolved and they want to speak out and are comfortable in speaking out. They want the world to know what went on for them, so they can change the world, because in order for healing to take place, you need justice and you need a voice. You need to speak out.

It was strange. There was a survey done about people that have been abused, where disease and cancers developed, and it was common to get them in the stomach because these events make you feel clenched in the stomach, you know? A lot of men were getting bowel disorders.

Women were getting womb cancer and things like that; ovarian cancer, because of the abuse. Another place was in the throat because they're not speaking out, they can't speak out and it's just repression and everything else, so it's about understanding victims.

Then you get others. People that have been hurt but go on to hurt and unfortunately, some of them have come my way and then they've gone out their way to cause a lot of problems. They've got inside the camp, as it were and then they've gone on to cause chaos.

Then you've got those that have never been part of the gang but hate me. They want to destroy me. They see me as a threat and they want to discredit me.

Cooper: Who do? Are we talking about the establishment at this point?

Wedger: Well, yeah, I mean some of it will be establishment-led, others will be satanic groups or will be paedophiles.

Cooper: Because they're all connected, right? So, I should imagine that they can all be against you, right?

Wedger: Yeah, and someone said to me, "you're going to get attacked by paedophiles and their protectors" because they can't have me speaking out.

You know, I'm one of the few... there are not many police whistle blowers. There are a few high-profile ones but when you look, and I'm not denigrating anyone, because again, bless them, they're brave but a lot of them, they spoke out once they retired. I spoke out once I was in post and it was very dangerous for me. It was a magnified level of danger that I put myself in.

So I want to go on about how the establishment will take you down, if you're not prepared to fight and this is about having the strength and fighting. This isn't a street fight. This isn't shirts off in a car park or anything like this. This is a spiritual battle. You're going to get spiritually attacked, you're going to get financially attacked and you're going to get your character assassinated. I've had my whole private life exposed and splashed all over, but I don't care because I don't do anything wrong.

I'm not interested in what anyone's got to say about me or trolling and all that. Really, I'm not bothered and it's funny when you see the people that do it, they're very vexed, they're hate-fueled, they're very dysfunctional, they're incredibly angry and they've got a problem.

But there are others that love me for what I do.

There are a lot of, like I said, very... what would have been dangerous people, they're behind me so much and I've been with one today and hopefully he'll come on the show. He's got a phenomenal story to tell.

Tomorrow, I'm with a former prostitute drug courier and she was a porn actress as well who was trafficked. I'm spending time with her and her friend, who's another very serious ex-gangster. And then, the next day I'm working with someone who deals with Voodoo, who's exposing Voodoo.

So this is what my time is but before I worked in a group. It collapsed because there was too much infighting. Too much spite and hatred, and all sorts of manner of emotions floating around and so I've gone back to how I started off, which was on my own.

I was told by a profiler I worked with, a brilliant woman... she is one of the FBI's top profilers. 10th in the world I think, in the top 10 for child murderers - a lady called Carine Hutsebaut and she said to me, "whatever you do, you work on your own. You work like a submarine, you go under, you come up, and then you go under again but you work alone. You'll be a link in a chain don't be part of a group". I can put you in touch with her.

There was an infamous child murderer, paedophile, procurer of children for satanic rituals called Marc Dutroux, in Belgium, and if you ever want to watch a great documentary, watch "The Beast of Belgium". I think BBC did a documentary on this man. He was procuring children for the government.

Cooper: Procuring for the *government* did you say?

Wedger: Kidnapping, hiding them in cellars, torturing them, pimping them out to sex parties, and then murdering them. It was all filmed and when it came out, there were members of the Royal Family in Belgium, the parliament, CEO's of businesses - all involved, and this will really dovetail into what I'll go on about.

This was in the 90's, this was the mid-90's and the good thing about what happened in Belgium, was they tried to cover it up, which the British establishment is phenomenal at doing, covering everything up... look the other way; "this is England, dear boy, this doesn't go on here". You know?

We'll blame the foreigners and we'll mock them but we'll never point the finger at our own, and we're seeing that with the Epstein thing and with Ted Heath and I can extensively cover a lot of that.

But they tried it in Belgium. Now, Belgium's not a big country and it's demographically very similar to the UK, an industrial country. I think we've got the same unemployment levels and things like that.

Cooper: I think they've got one of the highest suicide rates in Europe actually, in Belgium.

Wedger: Yeah, it's a rough country, it's a tough country. It's not just beer and chips. It's got a lot of problems. There are social problems and despite that, just short of a million people took to the

17

streets and protested. The firemen emptied their high-pressure hoses, on the parliamentary building, blew the windows out because they said this place needs cleansing, and they took to the streets and because of that, the world knew about it. Had they not, no one would have known.

But this lady Carine, I've worked very closely with her over the last few years. She profiled him and she goes and interviews child murderers and she's been a phenomenal insight into the criminal mind. More so, than what the police are doing.

One of the arms of my campaigning is that the police are educated properly and hopefully the government enquiry, which I was part of – they've asked me if I would like to have an advisory role in it and one of the things I said is, "I want to be part of the education for detectives and teaching them why people commit crime".

You know 80% of the Category C under 25 prison population come from abused childhood backgrounds. So, if we solve child abuse, we solve a lot.

Cooper: Do you trust them though? I mean, having come from that…

Wedger: No, but…

Cooper: Do you feel as though there still can be good work done in there?

Wedger: Always.

Cooper: Are there still good people in there that want to see this change or not?

Wedger: Yeah, always. You never give up. Someone said to me, "Jon, at the end of the day, what are you going to change?" And I said, "listen, put it this way, I'm never going to stop child abuse and I'll be an idiot to think I'm going to stop it, let alone satanic ritual abuse but if I'm a stone in their shoe, if I'm a biscuit crumb in their bedsheet…"

Cooper: …It's better than nothing.

Wedger: Yeah, a little mosquito bite on their neck. It's better than doing nothing. You can't do nothing because if you do nothing, children suffer.

But if we take this back to your original question. I joined the police in the early 90's and culturally and on every level, it was totally different to policing now. I've been away from the policing environment probably since about 2014, officially since 2017 because I actually walked out but remained still on their books in 2014. 2017 I retired and I've been a detective for a good portion of my career.

But I started on uniform policing like everyone. I started in South East London and the early 90's there was a problem with crack cocaine, and heroin. I wouldn't have thought it's changed much but there was a lot more poverty and street crime going on there. You had some very impoverished areas. London's getting heavily gentrified now. A lot of money's been ploughed in but back then it wasn't.

When I joined, they were going through a recruitment phase because they were starting to retire people. There was a big proportion of people getting retired. So, I was part of the... I don't know what they call it... "Operation Stable Door", in the police, this knee-jerk reaction; "shit, we haven't recruited enough people" so a lot of them when I joined have come from the 1960's and they had been very busy in the 70's and the 80's. So, they were violent some of them, it was tough.

Cooper: Were they thugs themselves some of them?

Wedger: Yeah, "hands-on". Which I'm not saying is a bad thing either. It's quite paradoxical because some parts of London, that's how it was, especially when I joined.

Cooper: Without CCTV, I'm guessing as well, you had to look after yourself a lot more right?

Wedger: There was no CCTV. They just brought in the "police and criminal evidence act" so a lot of coppers... these blokes worked "pre-pace", as they call it. So there were no prisoner's rights back then.

It was still their mindset in that era and a lot of the people when you dealt with them on the street, they expected it. So, it was a bit like a school fight. It's who gets the first punch in and it was just a street fight and it was one thing that got me, was the violence. I was thinking, it's unbelievable and it was like a war zone. But there was a bit of honour to them because it was only really when I got into my detective years when I started having knives pulled on me and things like that and stopped threats of firearms. However on a uniform copper side, you didn't really get that but people would want to get away and they would have a go at you. So it was fair cop you know, if you got the better of them, you'd have a drink with them sometimes.

Cooper: Yeah??

Wedger: Yeah, I remember being in a bar one day and a bloke come over and he said, "all right, officer?" and I'm thinking, "how does he know?"

He said to me, "do you remember the battle of Looper Street?" And I went, "oh, my god!"

It was a whole housing state versus us and one cop actually got slashed across the face, which was a bit naughty but yeah it was this big fight and we were just drinking and laughing about it, you know. Who hit who and who what where.

The coppers I found there were very brave. I'll talk on the positives and I will go on to the negatives. They were warriors. I was really impressed by the girls and the boys. But one of the things that hit me straight away is that the police teach you to lie.

Now, I'm not going to admit anything on here and it'll be up to people to read between the lines of this but on an evidence level there would be a protocol amongst the officers and there would be one strong leader within the team.

People think in the rank structure; the sergeants run it, and all that. Well not really. You'll have a senior copper, and the sergeants ask *him* the best way to do it.

We definitely had one of them. He was a fair bloke, he was a tough bloke but sometimes you go up and do your evidence and the senior copper throws down his evidence and says, "right, *that's* the evidence". *"That's the evidence"* and that's how it was, you know.

I'm not saying I was involved in that, I'm not saying I wasn't. But I mean so very soon you learned that this is the culture and if you don't abide by that, then that is it, you're ostracised.

Now, you must survive in the environment you're in. That's a given. It was in the era when corruption was starting to weed out. It was still quite rife, especially in the detective departments and I never really saw it until a couple of years in. You started seeing how it really worked and that was in the CID (Criminal Investigation Department).

I didn't really see corruption with uniform coppers, I saw a lot of lying. I saw a lot of people getting a slap. I would say eight times out of ten they deserved it, on other occasions they didn't, unfortunately.

Cooper: For the public you mean? Unfairly get a slap?

Wedger: Yeah, it was rare. It was rare but there were times when someone did deserve it. Unfortunately, what happens is that when you're in that environment - that violent environment, it becomes part of you and *you* become violent. And so, that's why coppers stick to their own because they understand each other, a bit like soldiers do.

Cooper: It's tribal, right? I guess when the uniform goes on, a different character comes out too.

Wedger: And you drink. You know there are not many non-drinkers.

Cooper: Right and I'm guessing if you don't drink, you're not part of the gang.

Wedger: No, you're not and that's that. However, one guy I worked with, he'd become an Imam.

Cooper: All right, good luck!

Wedger: Yeah, he was a drinker and a drug taker and all sorts and the next time I saw him, he'd become an Imam!

I went, "what!" He went, "them days are behind me now". You know with the beard, the cloak and everything so we had a little laugh about that, but the drinking culture is massive.

I didn't like the training, I hated the training. I hate regimentation. I couldn't stand it. It's really weird because they say it's a civilian police force. However, it's classed as a disciplined service so there's a bit of a paradox there with what it is, what it isn't.

The instructors, the PTI instructors were all ex-army guys, every single one of them and so they still had that ex-army regimentation. You had to march everywhere. We had members of the Coldstream Guards who would take us for the parade in the morning. So it was done to a military standard, so your uniform had to be perfect and you get the same sort of punishments for stupid things like a speck of dust and sometimes they'd have an inspector on parade and smudge your shoes and then the army guy would come along and then start screaming at you for your shoes being smudged.

Cooper: What was the reason for that? To toughen people up?

Wedger: I don't know, I never got it really, but the ex-army guys loved it. They creamed their pants over it. They were like, "oh no, it's really good". I hated it.

See with me, I hated marching, right? And watching even back in the tender years and watching everyone turn left to dismiss from parades, they'd say, "parade dismissed" or whatever their terminology was and they all turned to the left and they'd walk two paces and then stand to attention and then off you wander. Watching it all, when everyone's going to the classes, had to go as a group, marching. And you'd have the class captain doing this "left, right, left, right", stuff.

Cooper: I didn't know that went on.

Wedger: Yeah, it did back then. It was very strict and it made me feel sick because I thought, "wow, this is how Nazis are made". This is how indoctrination was done.

Cooper: Well, it's cult-like, isn't it?

Wedger: Yeah, and it is. It really is and it's this mantra and it starts getting under your skin.

I had a lot of self-discipline because I used to do a lot of exercise but I'm a loner. I was born a loner and I will die a loner. I like my own company.

I've always had quite a high IQ, like a comprehensive education but I could have done a lot more with it but the opportunities weren't there because at the time, I came from a single parent family.

My father died when we were young, my mum worked in a pub and that's how it was and I was just from a working-class area and with working-class friends but I always achieved everything, I always did.

I was always quite a good achiever but with the police, I struggled with the training because it was regimentation and I hated it. I hated every minute of it and what got me through was I was a good swimmer and the recruits weren't allowed to use the swimming pool. They had a beautiful swimming pool, but I used to think I'm just going in it. So, during the lunch break, I would just go swimming and the PTI said, "no, you're not allowed, you're a recruit". But I would do it, I kept going.

And he came up to me one day, he said, "listen, I've told you once and you'll be put on a charge" and if you got put on a charge you'd have to parade outside their drill office at six in the morning and they'd have an early morning parade.

It's just stupid crap but he said, "if you can swim a mile breaststroke in under 25 minutes, you can stay".

He said "but the condition is, if you do it, you have to attend wrestling lessons" because they had a wrestling club and he ran it and no one was attending.

He only had one bloke. He needed someone else to wrestle with him and I was in good shape. I looked after myself and all that.

So, I did. I swam a mile which is competitive level, county level. Probably better than that to be honest. He went, "well done". So he let me swim and it got me through the training, got me through and I ended up doing wrestling which *did* save my life, the wrestling because I became good at that.

Cooper: Is that normal to have wrestling, to toughen up the police and get them more sharpened for the street?

Wedger: Yeah, you see it in America. They use it a lot because everything ends up as a wrestle anyway. You know a few punches are thrown but on the whole, you can't go up to someone on the street and start jabbing them.

Cooper: It always ends up being a grapple.

Wedger: And it did, there were a couple of occasions when I could have been seriously hurt, had I not done this and it just taught me to get straight in there.

It was funny. It was a gypsy who said to me, "if anyone mouths at you, just jump on them but be careful of those that don't". And I went, "what are you on about" and with that, he punched me in the face. And I said, "why did you do that?" He said, "well, you didn't think I was going to do it". I said, "well, no you were quiet". He said, "*exactly*, just be careful that's all I'm saying".

And it's true with the police, that the mouthy ones…um…

Cooper: …The quiet ones are the ones that are about to spring.

Wedger: Yeah, "empty vessels make the most noise", as it were. They shout and scream and all that and "the squeaky wheel gets the oil", whereas… they found out with the paramedic teams when they arrive, if they're making a noise, their lungs are working, their hearts are beating and their circulatory systems are working because they're feeling pain. Leave them. Leave the mouthy ones screaming, the quiet ones are in trouble.

And it was really a metaphor for life in general because all the criminals I dealt with... and then I dealt with child abuse ultimately and these are the quiet victims and they've suffered the most. They suffered the most. Not someone who's had a slap off their husband.

(I'm not someone who's advocating domestic violence or anything like that and I'm always careful what I say because there's always a backlash with me. The trolls appear, I'll tell you. I get attacked more times than David Icke!)

But these are child victims and it's the same as people on the street, when you talk to them, the beggars and all of them, come from the care homes and that's a product of it, living on the street. You know with abscesses on your arms and a crack addiction - kids in care.

The whole destruction of it, yet they put no resources into it and they denigrate the victims and they denigrate the survivors and they silence them throughout the justice system.

Cooper: Who silences them?

Wedger: I'll come on to it. It's a bit of legislation called "The Bad Character Act". Part of the Criminal Justice Act of 2003.

Again, no doubt a troll will pick me up and say, it's actually 2000 and so on but it's how you can assassinate a character legitimately in a court and it just destroys everything and we've seen that with a few high-profile cases... paedophile cases when the victims have been not only attacked but sent to prison.

It starts very early on, this attacking character and it starts in the care homes, it starts in schools, and they can use all of this. [Deeming someone as a liar]

Cooper: So, if they don't like someone, they can put them through all that, can they?

Wedger: Well, if we jump the timeline... and I address this point you brought up here, John.

Someone who is harbouring a drug addiction. For men they will rob or they will steal, burgle houses or deal drugs or nick from shops or whatever. The more you get into the street drug scene, the more the heroin and the Class-A drugs take a hold. The more unsophisticated crimes get because you start losing it, you know?

So, someone that might have started off as quite an accomplished diligent criminal, will end up just as a crackhead stealing sandwiches out Marks and Spencer's because this is the need to do it.

Women... ultimately prostitution is something that will give them instant money very quickly for not much effort, do you know what I mean? So, it's a good way of paying the drug bill.

But why? Why is someone doing it, you might ask? Well, heroin is an analgesic. It's a painkiller. It's a suppressor of pain. Now, pain isn't just physical, pain is also emotional. And there was a study done where they found that 90% of the heroin addicts (I don't know where it was done, whether it was over here or abroad), had come from sexual abuse. There's a big correlation between heroin addiction and sexual abuse, childhood sexual abuse.

If you're nicking them... there's on the whole, a shoplifter who is going to get caught one time in a hundred. So, every time they get caught, that's it, they've had a result one way or another, but they get that on their record; shoplifting. That's a crime of dishonesty. So, it's going to go down on your sheets as dishonesty.

Now, at some point in the chronology of a person's life, and if they end up trusting a policeman or they want to do the right thing, they're going to say, "right, I've got to be honest with myself, why am I doing it?"

They may remember their time in the care home. They remember being abused at home. You know the police come in, they get put in a care home. Mum is no use, dad is an alcoholic or if there is a dad, you know?

And I really want to talk about this single-parent culture and I know it could upset people but I was a single parent. I feel I'm qualified to talk about single parenting and I really want to go into this because it's one big way of remedying this appalling situation of child abuse that we've got.

And then they start getting abused in the care home which is endemic especially back in the day the 60's, the 70's, the 80's. The care homes were endemic for abuse.

Cooper: Why is that though? I don't get that because surely an institution like that is meant to care for people. But why is it all inverted and just gets exploited?

Wedger: Kids are money and look, if you want a woman, you go to a pub. Not now because there's hardly any left but I mean back in the day you'd go in the pub and there are women in there, right? So, you're going to go where your sexual desire is.

If you're a paedophile, you've got to go where kids are. Now, paedophiles on the whole, don't have previous convictions. So, these CRB checks, these criminal record bureau checks are absolutely of no use whatsoever when it comes to child abuse issues.

They will always root out a violent person or a deceiver, right? Because on the whole, there is a chronology, a crime if you're violent. You start off punching someone at school and then whacking someone outside a pub and then using a weapon to hit someone, and blah de blah and then shooting, stabbing and whatnot.

Cooper: Yeah, it's a clear progression.

Wedger: There's a progression. On the whole.

The same with violence. You don't just think I'm going to get a gun and do an armed robbery. There would have been, again this chronology of criminality that's led up to that.

Paedophiles are deceptive people. They're patient people. Everything they do is well thought out, and well planned. And it's a cognitive distortion, how they twist things, how they become the victim, how they groom.

And grooming is no different and this might sound like sour grapes but how a guy who's good at chatting with women? What does he tell her? He just wants to have sex with her, right? And that's it because that's how men are and that's what they do.

Women aren't built the same as men. There might be one or two but on the whole they want to go out for a drink and these blokes are like, "right, I want to have sex".

So, they're going to tell that woman everything she wants to know. They're going to tell her how she smells nice, how she looks nice, and this and that and then he gets his prize, and then he's off to the next one and to the next one.

He's a player, that's how it works and that's how it's always worked. Very similar traits... and I'm not saying that players are paedophiles, I'm not. I'm just putting an analogy out there so people can understand the process.

A groomer… now it's not a monster that grooms a child, it's a kind man that grooms a child (or woman and I want to go on about females and paedophilia). They're nice. They're endearing but they've got an agenda and their agenda is to have sex with that child and not just have sex with that child.

Cooper: They're not really kind. They're putting a persona on.

Wedger: Yeah of course. Luckily I was one of the very few coppers that got trained in profiling. It wasn't to a degree standard but it was hands-on… I worked with one of the best profilers in the UK back then; a guy that was based in Southern Ireland and I learned so much from him.

One of the videos when they were working with paedophiles and it's all to do with grooming - how grooming works and they put a guy in a chair and they sit him down and another paedophile's job was to convince him to get off the chair. Whatever it takes, get him off that chair. No violence, no nothing.

So, he will tell him, "Hello mate", yeah, it was all nice… "come and stand up to see what you look like".

The other guy's brief was just to do his best to stay in that chair.

And, of course, he doesn't, he doesn't move. He doesn't do it but this fellow is nice, he's offering him a cigarette, he's offering some chocolate, and ultimately, the paedophile can't control himself, right?

Then he flips and the monster comes out and then the next thing you watch in this video (and it was so consistent with all the people that were put in the scenario) and once he's had enough, he's had enough and he just tears into the bloke who was on the chair.

31

He said, "that's what happens when the child doesn't acquiesce". The monster comes out.

So, it's not a "monster" that grooms a child. These paedophiles are monsters though obviously, they are monsters. They're evil.

I interviewed a very high-profile child murderer once… a woman and I've become a specialist interviewer. I've got a natural ability to communicate, and luckily the police recognised it. One of the good things they *did* do and they exploited it. I'm glad they did because it took me all over the place doing all sorts of things and ultimately teaching these skills.

And the same with this woman… she was endearing, she was nice, she was all that but then the moment I cross-examined her and the moment… because there is a skill when you get into that level of interview and it is neuro-linguistic programming, that part of it and a lot of it is understanding how people work.

And that was it, she just kicked off. The moment she realised she'd been rumbled, she called me a "C U Next Tuesday", spat in my face, and just went mad. And it happened like that and I said, "there you go, that's the monster your son sees". And even the solicitor was just dumbfounded.

Cooper: Yeah, because that's the thing, people don't realise, there are plenty of female paedophiles. We have this image of the paedophile being like the outcast white…

Wedger: …middle-aged white man.

Cooper: Nerd. Middle-aged nerd, right?

Wedger: …living with his mum. A bit of a loner. Very polite like the Thomas Hamilton, the Dunblane murderer but it's not.

And this is one of the things that I set out to do and I tried to do this in the police, to change what a paedophile looks like.

I dealt with paedophiles that were Kosovan, Albanian refugees, good-looking guys. Like young Italian lads, young Jamaican guys, Greek guys, white guys, mixed race guys. Young, in their 20's and 30's, having sex with young kids. And same with women too.

The one thing you'll find with women is a deception that a man can't attain. There is a level of spite and deception that goes along with women and abuse.

Cooper: Yeah? So, what are they doing to the kid? I don't want to go too much into it, but I kind of need to know this. What levels are these women going to? Molesting or…

Wedger: Yes, sexually abusing. I mean there was one woman who was getting her child and she was getting the feet of the child and she was putting them up her vagina and sort of re-enacting the birth of the child.

One woman was putting like sugary stuff on her vagina and getting her little baby… because babies they've got a natural ability to suckle… and so instead of breastfeeding the baby, she was putting it on her clitoris and the baby was doing that.

One guy was in a care home and he said that the men were abusing him but he said that the women were the worst and he said;

"There were loads of us, young boys from 6 to 13 and every day, *every* day we'd have to go to the school hall, we all had to strip off

33

naked, so you're getting prepubescent boys… we'll all have to line up and the Headmistress of the school would sit there and make all the girls of this residential school watch. (They were all clothed) while she took us one by one. She'd cane us, and fiddled with our genitals and then off we went to get changed and then get ready for our evening meal. Every night that went on, *every* night".

Cooper: In the care home?

Wedger: In the care home. *Every* single night.

I've heard of people having their genitals whipped. One guy told me… it was so sad… he was a lovely man. He helped the survivors, a lovely old man and there was a pain in his voice.

I said, "what's your story, my friend?" He went, "no, I just help". I said, "why? Everyone's got a reason for doing this". And he said, "well, I was in a care home and I was made to strip naked and a woman teacher would whip my penis with a ruler so badly that it ruptured and I could never get an erection".

What was sad about this, he was 80 years old this man, an old man telling me and he said, "what was the sad thing about this is… and back then you never had sex until you were married and you would court a girl, you'd take a girl out and I was in love. I wanted to marry this girl, she loved me and I loved her but I couldn't get an erection and we planned marriage and I jilted her because I knew that I could never sexually give her what she wanted and I had to run away. I was too… I didn't have the balls… it was too much and I did it, not for me but for her because I would never be able to sexually please her. I'd never be able to have sex with her because my penis wouldn't work in that way because it'd just been whipped mercilessly by that woman with a ruler when I was a boy".

And the satanic abuse takes that to an even darker level that takes it to a murdering level. If we could go into that...

Cooper: Yes, so we have paedophilia and that permeates, I would say almost all institutions. It's there everywhere, right? But then it goes into more of the darker aspects of paedophilia, right? Is there a kind of link between it all or two separate things?

Wedger: Yeah, you'll find a lot of the problems in society are down to paedophilia. A lot of them. And what you have in society, you have economic crime. They give it all these stupid names now but on the whole, it's a reserve of the lower and the working classes, the council estates, right?

Cooper: Yeah, petty crimes.

Wedger: Car thieving, burglary, people robbing their own people, mugging each other and all that. It's brain damage crime. It's idiotic, stupid, poverty-driven crime.

However, paedophilia is different. Paedophilia knows no social boundaries. It knows no religious boundaries. It knows no economic issues. It just knows no gender issues. It is like a hot knife through the butter of society, it cuts through everything and it will unite so many people and that's why you will see organised criminals, knowing MP's. That's why you have MP's knowing prostitutes. That's why all these MP's will know lower class people and you think how do they know each other?

Cooper: Can I just ask before we go into it, what is it about children that's so appealing as opposed to just a prostitute you think?

Wedger: Children, it's all about power. They enjoy sex with children. These are damaged people that get an immense amount of pleasure from having sex with a child. It invigorates them.

If we stick with a man, a man having sex with a seven-year-old girl this isn't a man that could pleasure a grown woman. There's a problem there; a deep-rooted mental, cognitively distorted issue going on. They enjoy it. They enjoy the pain it gives them, the fear it gives them and…

Cooper: Pain it gives them?

Wedger: Yeah, well, the pain it gives to the child.

Cooper: Oh, the pain it gives the child, yeah…

Wedger: They enjoy it. I said to one guy I said, "right come on now, what is it? What is it?"

And he said, "I remember being in a flat with three other paedophiles and we wanted to get a boy, right?" And he said, "have you ever seen a heroin addict without any drugs?"

I said, "oh, all the time".

He said they were pacing. Pacing up and down and then the mobile phone went and the call came from the fellow that was out scouting for a kid. I don't know where he was procuring it from and he said,

"I've got us a boy" and he said it was like a pressure cooker letting the valve open, and everyone relaxed.

Cooper: Oh, God.

Wedger: And he said when you have sex with that boy, you felt high, you felt invigorated, and it's food for them. These are people that enjoy what they do.

Cooper: Is there any preference? Do they prefer a boy to a girl, these paedophiles?

Wedger: Yeah, they will have a preference. But what they call paedophiles – they're "tri-sexual". They're not homosexual, they are not bisexual, they're trisexual. They will try anything.

So, again, we'll just stick with men. I will come on to the women. I reserve a little place for the women when I deal with the satanic stuff and what they've been involved in.

With a man, he may like pre-pubescent, pre-seven-year-olds... the age means a lot as well. Some like *babies*.

We saw that with Ian Watkins, the Lost Prophet singer abusing babies and a lot of his files have been locked away for *40* years. Why?

So, he'll like a seven-year-old pre-pubescent girl. But he'll have sex with a teenage boy. But that's what he likes. They've got their demographic, what they want, what they prefer but they are a danger to all children, *all* children they're a danger to.

37

And the strange thing is, if I go back to my early years in the police, it was never formed part of the training. We did four days on dangerous dogs and racial issues.

I never saw corruption in the uniform. I saw stupidity in the uniform branch, I saw ego-driven morons really.

CID (Criminal Investigation Department), I saw corruption. Racism, I'm saying no. This is going to shock people... NO. Not on my level.

It went on, of course. It was no different to racism that I saw... in fact, it was less than the racism I saw when I was doing my apprenticeship, when I was at evening college... when I was working on building sites.

The building sites were a lot more racist than the police. Without a doubt. It was effing this and effing that and sexist and there's no way you'd get away with that in the police. The police were too regulated. And I never saw homophobia either. There was banter and there was *raw* banter but everyone was part of it. The gay officers would be part of it. The Jamaican officers would be part of it and like I always said the ones who got picked on the most were the gingers.

Cooper: Yeah, I know! They're the ones that don't get any support!

Wedger: No one supported them. So, gingerphobes got away with it but I never saw racism but then again, why would I? I'm not a black officer.

I got called gypsy a lot because they thought I was a gypsy. A senior officer once asked me if I would like to challenge it and because some officer called me a pikey and I was like, I don't care. I am not bothered.

There's also sectarianism. They don't tend to like Catholics going anywhere. We've got a very Protestant police force and if you go to Glasgow, Strathclyde, it's all Protestants, *all* Protestant. So, there's a lot of sectarianism.

There's a lot of Masonry…and Masonry has a massive steer, well, it did back then.

Cooper: Shall we tangent off into that quickly or did you want to bring it round to what you were just talking about?

Wedger: Well, I never encountered Masons. I didn't know what Masonry was, to be honest. I'd heard of them and they would just call them the "Larry's". "The Larry Grayson's" - The Masons.

It would be mentioned and it was never really until I start working with older coppers and they'd say, "oh, he's in my lodge". And I was like, "what's that mean?" And then I started knowing about it.

Then I ended up on a specialist department. I specialised quite a lot, which was brilliant. Some people never specialise, and some do it once. I did it many times, and I definitely saw it as a way forward. I loved it, going on to specialist departments but Masonry was endemic, absolutely endemic in them and they all knew each other, and they were all connected with each other. There were people who would get jobs and you wouldn't know how.

Cooper: They'd be fast-tracked because they're part of it?

Wedger: Always. They'd be picked for this and picked for that and they were useless, inept, moronic, lazy, whatever and it was never really done on merit in the police. I never saw people really promoted on merit.

There were those that did but they had to work hard, I was one of them. I had to work hard for what I got. But I was just very good at policing. I was just naturally good at it.

Some people are naturally good at gymnastics, some are naturally good boxers... I was good at that and it caused a lot of jealousy.

And then one day, I went for a job and this was the first time I've been silenced. I was tracking down transient paedophiles that were living on canal boats and it was a cracking number and a lot of the older lads were all Masons. This was the first time I started seeing it and a few of them would have a ring [on one finger].

One used to wear a watch with... what's the Jewish language?

Cooper: Hebrew.

Wedger: Hebrew, because it's all to do with Solomon. There's a lot of Jewish references.

It's all to do with King Solomon's temple or something like that. And so there'll be a lot of Hebrew inscriptions on his watch and that was always masonic and a handshake would give it away. They'd do a knuckle rub thing, where they'd rub their knuckles, depending on what level they were.

Cooper: How many of the police do you think were Freemasons? They weren't all overt?

Wedger: I don't know. I know that if you take things like the dog unit. Probably maybe 70-80% were.

Cooper: 70/80%?!

Wedger: Yeah, the male ones. Women aren't allowed to. When I was in the vice unit, I'd say a good half of the men were Masons.

But I was on this one job tracking down paedophiles and it got so big... it was absolutely massive. I was expected to locate two paedophiles in two months. I located ninety and it started then moving on to some politicians who were involved with it and it got shut down and they said, "right, you're off this unit. It's shutting down but you can have any job you want". I said, "well, I want to stay here, I want to go and do this and I said why?" They said, "well, we haven't got the funding for it".

In the end, I was told it came from high up; "Shut him down, back him down". And then I got told by a senior officer at the paedophile unit at Scotland Yard; "you trod on toes. You got very good at what you did and they came for you".

So, it was the first time but it wasn't going to be the last time.

Cooper: That was the first moment that you went, "hang on a minute, there's something going on here".

Wedger: Yeah. I was seconded to the paedophile unit. I was on the river police and I was tracking down transient paedophiles that were living on canal boats because they had a loophole...

Cooper: So it wasn't a complete cover-up. They would still send officers in to deal with paedophiles?

Wedger: Well, it was the fact that information was coming from the prisons and there was pressure to track down transient paedophiles. They didn't know where they were…

Cooper: What do you mean by "transient?"

Wedger: Well, they're not signing on the sex offenders register because they just brought in the sex offenders register in 1997 and these paedophiles were just going missing. They were going all over the place. We didn't know where they were and there was information because the police work on informants, on that level, on that sort of detective level it's all informants and the information was coming from the paedophile community in prison, when you get out, they got the sex offenders register.

They'd say, "They can't catch you. If they catch you, they monitor you, if they monitor you, they can come into your house and if they come into your house, game's over for us all so don't get on that register".

So, they had 28 days to register themselves on release or conviction or caution for schedule 1 sexual offence and they weren't doing it.

And now, if you get on a canal boat, police don't go on canals and canals – they're on boundaries, they form boundaries, borough boundaries.

So, London's very unique as much as we've got one police force. Well, we've got two police forces in London.

We've got the city of London which is very bizarre because the city of London doesn't sign allegiance to the Queen. They're not linked to the crown.

The only police force in the commonwealth that doesn't have the King Edward's coronet, the crown that you see on the badges. They've got griffins. They're to do with some financial thing.

And Parliament has no control and the Queen [now the King] has no control over the city of London police at all. Yeah, very, very bizarre bunch. Really odd.

So funnily enough, I had that when I was meeting with a parliamentarian for police and crime and he turned around and said, "we've got no power over them".

I said, "when I say it's a conspiracy…" He went "no, no no, you're right, I can't tell him what to do. I can tell every other chief constable what to do or advise him what to do but I can't tell that lot anything. We've got no power over the city of London".

Very odd. So you've got all these other county forces; Hertfordshire, Bedfordshire, Cambridgeshire, and all that. They're their own entity.

London is made up of different boroughs and each one, is in effect its own little police force, right? So, each one is its own police district.

So, you could have a canal boat on the river Lea and to the left, you could have Waltham Forest, to the right you could have Hackney and to the north, you could have, I don't know, Enfield and it'll all be within five minutes.

So, he could flip about. So 28 days he's got to register as a sex offender, he just moves over there, and doesn't have to register.

And kids like boats and a lot of these sex offenders were setting themselves up as respite carers for special needs kids. There was one, he was working for a tour company taking children from

Camden town on school trips to London Zoo on a canal boat and he was put in charge of toilet patrols.

He was a prolific paedophile and he was a young lad and he was actually a good-looking lad. The girls would have liked him but he liked little girls.

So they were everywhere. Anyway, it just exploded. It's massive information. It was coming in from all around the world as soon as I put myself out, that's what I was doing. It was just filtering in and I didn't realise how big it was. It was just incredible and it got shut down very quickly.

And I said, "I want to carry on working with kids".

At the time, the vice unit wanted to advertise officers to join the vice unit again. It was an elite unit, a brilliant unit.

They went all around the world. They dealt with casino crime, they dealt with prostitution, they dealt with nightclubs. Oh, man, it was a one to have and it was like plain clothes posting and I thought well, I'll have that.

It was very hard to get on back then and this is when I first saw Masonry.

The guy that I've been working for was a Detective Sergeant. He was a Mason and he said, "where's the advert for this job?" and I showed him.

And he saw applications to "Inspector so and so". He went, "he's in my lodge". I went, "what's that mean?" He went, "you watch"… rings him up and he said, "look, I've got a lad applying for that job" and you can hear him saying, "yeah, he's a good kid. He's a really good kid".

Cooper: ...but he's not in the lodge!

Wedger: "He's not on the square", they used to say but because I worked hard for this guy, he liked me. So, he said, "I'm prepared to sponsor you".

The next thing, he goes and gets a pen and paper, he's on the phone and he just writes down a few lines.

He went, "see you at the next meeting". The phone goes down and he passes me this note and he goes, "right, there's every single question you're going to be asked and there's the answer". And that's how it worked.

Cooper: And you had to abide by the set answers?

Wedger: Well, they give you, what they call a reading list and they say you're going to be asked questions, you don't know what they are. You go for an exam, in effect. You go before a panel and they might ask a question and if you haven't revised the legislation...

So, when you go for a specialised position, you've got to swot up on *all* the legislation. So, you have to know all the laws about this, maybe firearms, you need to know about guns and all that, and then they train you as well but you need to show a willingness and you need to be capable when you get in there and also certain areas you work, they would like you to know that area of London as well. So, you can't say, "I don't know where I'm going". Well, it's not good enough. You're a part of this team, you behave like part of the team.

So, I was given all these answers. He was like, "right, don't let me down" and I just walked it, just walked straight through it.

So, I'd gone from uniform policing... I went from South East London to the West End.

In the meantime, my missus at the time had left me and left me with four children. So, I'm now bringing up four kids on my own. She had problems... deep-rooted problems and that was it, I was left on my own. Didn't get a penny from anyone. The older two weren't even my kids. We were going to put the oldest one in care because he was a bit wild, should we say, because he'd had a rough time, not off me but beforehand.

So, I went through four years at a family court on a personal level and I took on these kids. Never got anything from the courts because I didn't qualify for anything. So, it's hard for me, it was hard for me and the poor boys, it was tough for them as well.

But I kept my private life separate from my work. I never went to welfare or anything but I was working hard, and luckily I had a good family that did step in and help. Good friends that stepped in and helped. So, I got through it. So, I understand single parenting and I understand the anguish of kids when there is a parent missing and my boys grew up without a mum and the youngest boy was nine months. So, it was hard for him. It was hard for me but again, it's not always about me.

I had an understanding of kids. But the last thing I wanted to do was work with kids because I was dealing with my own kids but then I started realising there is a correlation between crime and what the kids have suffered.

Then there was a fella early in my service. I was a jailer one night helping out in the cells and he said, "can I have a cigarette?" and I always took people out for a cigarette, always. It kept them quiet, I always give them a cup of tea and a cigarette. Others wouldn't, saying they don't believe in smoking and they were just snobs.

I said to them, "well, why are you on heroin? What's it about?" He said, "If you had my life, you'd be doing drugs. I went, "what do you mean? What do you mean?" He went, "I was in a care home and I was raped in a care home". And I went, "how old were you?"

And he was a young kid and he went through this awful story and he said, "I ended up in trouble and getting hit a lot at school because back then they could hit you (the teachers) and it just made it worse and I just had all the pain so I was drinking and then I did cannabis and then I went on to do ecstasy and heroin, and then off I went, a smack head and then I just spent my life burgling houses, but it was all down to the abuse".

So, very early on I realised that this is important.

Cooper: It's the root of it all.

Wedger: The root of it yet there was no education. Child protection was seen as a job for lactating mums.

So women that have come back from maternity leave, are shoved on child protection. They did sod all to help them. I'm not denigrating. At the end of the day, if they want to address a balance then they come on and they address a balance.

I'm going to say it as I experienced it and there were some good women I worked with and well, I'm not going to rubbish a whole swathe of people but there are others that were absolute snobs.

There were a lot of women on child protection who had no children. So what would they know about kids? They didn't understand poverty. They were married to coppers so they had the income of a middle-class family. They were living in middle-class areas because there was a financial incentive if you bought a house in a posh area.

I lived on a shit council estate, full of idiots. Again, I'm not knocking people living in council estates, I'm telling it as it was. And it was just a horrible place I was living on because that's all I could afford. I had a mortgage. I was living in poverty.

My kids went to the worst school in the area with problem families and everything and I had a crackhead prostitute living opposite me. I was burgled. Oh, it was just horrible. It was just an absolute nightmare. But then I was going to work with people that would go on all-inclusive holidays to Kenya that had Vogue SE Range Rovers.

I had more in common with the prisoners I was bringing through than the people I was working with!

Cooper: Maybe that's why it took you on this path.

Wedger: 100%. Actually, one of the criticisms that actually came out of the government inquiry… I think it might have been into the Victoria Climbie thing, was snobbery.

And it's something I brought up when I was given evidence at the government enquiry, late last year, it was the snobbery element. And this was basically it, that they were middle class people that just didn't want anything to do with the lower classes.

And there was one woman who wouldn't do a home visit, because she thought she would get scabies. She thought she'd get scabies off this council flat family and take it back to her precious little darlings that were living in the outskirts or wherever, you know, Bromley or whatever it was.

They were terrific snobs. Very rare would you get a really down-to-earth, street sort of person joining the police. It was very, very rare.

So that was a failing on one level, but only one level. I was later to find out that there were bigger failings because there was a concerted effort by Chief Constable level and military intelligence level to prevent disclosure of abuse, especially in institutional care homes, like Beach Home, which was down in Wandsworth, where kids were taken to Elm Guesthouse, which was down in Barnes and they were pimped out to MP's.

I was told mainly Tory MP's back in the day but it…

Cooper: But it knows no bounds.

Wedger: It's inter-party. It's inter-party, who were having sex with young boys.

I've been told of one fella, where he and his twin sister were taken to Elm Guesthouse as young as five-year-olds, and made to perform sexual acts on each other, while there was one politician in the room and there was a high court judge there and then they will rape them and then make them have sex with each other.

Cooper: With a high court judge you say?

Wedger: I was told he's still presiding now in the Crown Court circuit.

One guy, he was anally raped, he was beaten as a young boy and then taken to sex orgies, where numerous men would anally rape him and he said one of the men was his parole officer.

One was the Crown Court judge who later sentenced him to an armed robbery.

One was the social worker that was putting him in there.

So where did these kids turn? They've got *nowhere* to turn.

Cooper: No wonder they end up with a bit of escapism through the drugs. It kind of makes sense, doesn't it?

Wedger: It's only when you pick the scab, you realise this.

So I was working with people who are going on about, "I want to get on a Flying Squad, organised crime and all that".

Well, The Flying Squad, what do they do? They protect the banks, in essence. They're like a little unit in the police that just deal with bank robberies and bookies.

Well, bookmakers cause so much poverty. Casinos cause incredible amounts of poverty and so do banks. Banks make people homeless, and yet they get the cream, the so-called cream of the British police and unlimited funding, whereas those that are out there protecting children, you get just put down, silenced and attacked.

So I went on to the vice unit and I was dealing with street prostitutes to start with and I did very well there, I really enjoyed it.

All the prostitutes had all come from the care system and had all been sexually abused. Everyone I spoke to had been sexually abused every single one. They're all harbouring crack cocaine and heroin addictions. So they all come from the care homes.

So I started working with a couple of them. They would become my informants. And then they started giving me information about who was using them and then they started saying, "there's kids, there's kids involved, and some of the clients want us to get kids or the other street girls are procuring their children, or their family's children".

Cooper: Were they happy to give you this information because I'm supposing that they were part of that network and making money from it? So wasn't there a little bit of a conflict of interest?

Wedger: They only got paid if there was a conviction. But there were other ways of helping them.

You could get them to rehab centres, and things like that. You could leave them alone, you know, so they could work basically with impunity, and you wouldn't touch them, or you'd pick them up, make out you'd nick them and drop them around the corner, things like that.

You can make life easy for them. If they give information that resulted in conviction, they got paid. But on the whole, a lot of information they gave, wasn't financially viable, but a lot of them, they did it because they didn't like what was going on and they would also tell us about coppers.

They'd say, "there's policemen come here and pick up the girls as well".

And so I started working with that information. And then I was moved on very quickly. And I worked on casino crime, investigating casino crime, which was incredible. Just two of us in the whole world.

The majority of it was perpetrated by Turkish gangsters.

Cooper: Any paedophilia, or not?

Wedger: Just cheating casinos. So I got taken out on there. I ended up going back to working with children because I started dealing with the Turkish mafia and there was an attempt on my life.

Because I'd caused a lot of problems and seized a lot heroin, right? I was being used by the National Crime Squad to get information because some of the people started talking to me and giving me information about heroin importation, which then led me into serious and organised crime.

I would be sent into the prison system to interview gangsters in the prison who were giving me information and there was a trade, for liberty and for money if they gave the right information. So I started dealing with informants on like a national level and it ended up going to this international level, because some of the stuff was going abroad.

But then there was an attempt on my life. So I was moved away from that very quickly.

I ended up being asked to make an investigation into a young girl who would come forward and her name was Zoe. I can name her because she's dead. And I'll be dedicating part of my book, the autobiography, to this girl because very, very brave young girl that came from the care system. And she'd reported that she was being pimped out many times, to the police, and they just ignored her.

She was persistent. She kept coming forward. But she was heavily involved with organised crime and she was only about 14.

Again, this is a problem with the police as well. They put a lot of emphasis now on brothels but you're dealing with adults and to be honest, a lot of adults have a choice.

That might not be the case with some of the human trafficking but in my experience with vice, the girls that come over from Lithuania,

Latvia, and that, they'd worked in brothels in France, and in Italy and Germany, and then they made it here, and then they make an allegation that they've been exploited, but it was just a financial dispute between them and their pimp, on the whole, and so there wasn't any exploitation element, they just used it to their advantage.

It was en vogue to show this as some Russian mafia exploitation of women from the Eastern Bloc over here, like a Taken film with Liam Nielsen. Absolute bullshit. That weren't the reality. That was *not* the reality.

But under the veneer of that, were children. *Children* were being taken to brothels. *Children* were being taken to private venues. *Children* were being put on the street. And no one had looked into it. And whenever the kids came forward, they were told to go away.

Now, one girl about a year previous to me taking this investigation on... we picked her up in Market Road, in Islington. It was a red-light area back then. It's just up by Pentonville Prison, and she was 14. She was on crack cocaine. She was very small but because of a shit diet and living that lifestyle, she looked 10 or 11 and she's out there on the street, loitering, prostituting and whatever you call it.

By the way, I get attacked... "Jon Wedger calls them prostitutes", they say. Well, it is what it is. I mean, I'm here for the children, not against them.

And she had scabies, and a lot of them had a contagious thing like hepatitis, tuberculosis.

Going on about all this scare now with COVID; this "pandemic", but what about tuberculosis? It's massive. It's a huge problem and it's contagious. That *is* contagious.

So I put her in the car, and said I picked up so and so... and it came on radio, "get rid of her. She's got scabies. She will infect the car, the car will be off the road, and then that's you stuck in the office dealing with her".

And if we take her back to the office, we'd let them smoke. There was a room in a police station where they were allowed to smoke. 14 year olds - we'd give them fags and let them smoke.

It was mad back then. They said, "don't take her back to that room at Charing Cross police station, because she will infect that as well. Get rid of her". That was the attitude.

Now anyone who had sex with that girl, that was rape. That's 30 years. So really? Instead of a man picking up a prostitute, for a 50 quid fine, which wasn't even schedule 1 offence, so it wasn't a serious offence. It was a low-level C crime, the bottom crime.

So anyway, low level, they were interested in that but when you got a high-level crime like this - a rape of a child, they weren't interested.

So this is how the system works and it's never been about the people and all that.

I'll go back to Zoe in one sec because this is where it all started for me.

The police was formed in 1798. It was a Marine Police of London. And what was happening was that the Empire was big and the boats were coming in from all over the planet into what was called a pool of London, which was sort of East End of London and Tower Bridge and the docks were built, and the ships were there and they were moored up and they started to spoil some of the goods, there was a need to get these boats moving. But when the sailors went ashore, for night leave, especially in the East End, they were murdered, because the East End was rough and it was bad lands back then. And they were killed. And they were losing so many sailors for robberies, murders and everything else, that the shipping company said we're relocating to Amsterdam, we're not coming into London, it's too dangerous. You sort this out.

So they set up a paramilitary police force and they basically recruited Royal Marines because they had a good reputation and they were tough. So they drafted a load of Royal Marines and that's why the police used to have the big collars, the "boot-neck" as they called them, that's why they call the Royal Marines "boot-neck".

So they were just hard men, and they were put in there and they were told go out there and anyone robbed a ship, they'd die and that's that, and so it was all based on commerce and it was all based on commerce of the sea, because all they had was maritime law, so when they set up the courts, the first court was Thames Magistrates Court, which was on the Thames back then. It's not now.

It was all based on maritime law. That's why they stand in a dock. That's why it gets bailed out because if a boat is in trouble, you bail it out. So it's all to do with that.

Cooper: Even when you send something, it's "shipped". There's all these water-based terms.

Wedger: "Your wor*ship*". The bench is like the bridge of a boat, it's three steps up, so a judge has three steps up on the bench. It's all based on that.

Cooper: So, it's not the law of the land. It's the law of the sea.

Wedger: Yeah, you know, the boys in blue, and that's it. So it was all based on that. When they say it was conspiracy, all this about the economy. Well, it's not. Because the energy that something was built on in its inception, is the energy that stays with it. So that was built between a dispute between the trader and the merchant, and that still stands today.

It's got nothing to do with kids, or anything and protecting the vulnerable. It's all to do with protecting trade.

And it was interesting, what someone said to me about incest. The laws on incest, and they're really weird, right? So they said, "why is it not against the law for a grandmother to have sex with a grandson, yet a grandfather can't have sex with his granddaughter. It doesn't make sense".

Well it depends on your way of thinking. On a moral sense, of course, it doesn't make sense. It's perverted. Why would a grandson have sex with his grandmother, or the other way round.

But when you look at it on the fact that a grandfather, he has sex with his granddaughter, he could get her pregnant, and it's gonna cause a birth defect that's gonna maybe cause Down Syndrome that's gonna maybe cause numerous amounts of birth defects because of the gene pool.

But a young boy can't get an old woman pregnant because she's classed as "barren". She's over 50, the menopause. It's not much chance of him getting her pregnant so it's got absolutely nothing to do with perversion.

It's all to do with, is this child going to grow up to be a healthy member and productive member of society? Well, if not, then we have to outlaw it because everyone else has to pick up the bills. It's all still to do with money.

And the same with these kids' homes. Kids are moved about from home to home because they're traded like slaves were traded. So when slaves were traded, when they were shipped from here, they were sold to them and then when they moved from this plantation to that plantation, it was always a trade of money.

Because human beings have always been the ultimate commodity. Same as the children's homes, there's money every time a kid has moved from home to home, there's a trade in cash, so it makes money.

So these kids homes were making big money, they were getting two grand per week, per child. It was all about finance. So they weren't there to protect the kids, and give them the best and give them a good education and all that. They weren't.

Cooper: And I'm guessing there must be good people that work within there, but they just can't do anything. Right?

Wedger: What can you do when you're in a corrupt system?

Cooper: And that's exactly what happened to you, right?

Wedger: So this little girl Zoe turned round to me and said, "Look, I'm being pimped out". She was being pimped out by a woman who had a street name called Foxy.

Foxy was a street prostitute, who the police had known about for a long time. It was always rumours in intelligence reports that she was involved with young girls for a long time. And they did nothing. They did *nothing* to curtail it. Absolutely nothing.

She said, "it's not just me, there's other girls".

So when you see there was this drama, about three girls in the north, it was called Three Girls. It's about the grooming gangs in the north of England - three girls, which is terrible. But, you know, we had *dozens*.

Cooper: It must have been rife in London.

Wedger: One day I found 10 in one day, 10 kids in one day, in prostitution. I think the thing in Manchester, they had an incident room, a whole squad. We had two of us!

One girl led to another girl, led to another girl, then there were boys being involved, kids homes, and it was spiralling, and it was getting bigger and bigger and bigger. And then names start coming out and the people that were involved, and it was getting higher and higher and higher.

And then there was a threat that came in on my life. There was an intelligence report on my life.

And there was a social worker came forward from Croydon and she said, "Look, I hear what you're doing in North London and Central London, you've gotta help us in the South, we've got the same. We've been going to your unit" (who was set up to deal with juveniles at risk). They never, they just didn't touch them.

And she said, "but we've been going to them for a decade. There's girls, they're dying. There's boys that are dying".

There's one lad who was in the latter stages of HIV. He was 11. He was still being pimped out.

There was one girl, her vagina was so infected, that she had open cysts in there and she was *still* being pimped out and the social worker said when she would visit us, there was puss just oozing out of her legs, and she's still being pimped out and they'd say, "we go to your unit, and they do nothing. She's gonna die".

So I drafted a report and said look, this is the reality. We need to really stamp on this. This is just growing bigger and bigger every day.

And I was dragged down…

I've got to be careful because I'm in civil court against the Met Police in a couple of months. I'm suing them for their failures. I've had the government enquiry, which I've given evidence about their failures. So it's been heard, but again, I still gotta be careful.

I'm not going to name anyone but I was dragged in before the senior officer there, who's now gone on to be one of the most senior officers in the UK.

And he said to me, "what you done, what you done Jon? Listen, you're a good lad. You're well-liked and you're good at what you do but I'm telling you what, you mention a word of what you found out outside this room, you're gonna lose your home, your job and your children. You shut the eff up".

I knew he meant it.

I didn't mind the bloke, he was a nice bloke. He was well liked but he changed and I realised I'd trodden on some big toes here. He said, "You have no idea who or what you're dealing with. This is *so* big, you'll be thrown to the wolves and no one can help you. You must listen to me".

And he said, "You must promise *never* ever to look into this again".

Now, I didn't listen to him. I did the opposite to him and in due course, I nearly did lose my home, my job and my children *and* my liberty and I will explain how.

I was removed from that that enquiry. It went to court. Foxy was convicted. She was given 15 years, I think. Something like that.

She was the first conviction under the new legislation for grooming, and for pimping out kids. Again, a woman. A woman paedophile. She'd been active for a long time.

But the saddest thing is, that the little girl Zoe at the centre of it, she was found dead under suspicious circumstances very shortly afterwards and that broke me, that really broke me because she wasn't protected this girl. She was so brave and her efforts went a long way to opening this up, the way it has done.

And so, you know, I always have a little moment of prayer for that poor girl, and what she went through, and the system let her down, the social services, let her down. The police monumentally let her down and it shows it's broken, it doesn't work.

But I went on to work with child protection in Harringay, in North London. I found by the end of one week, 50 kids who had been pimped out.

I put a job together to sort of deal with it.

These are kids that were in care homes that were just being taken to brothels and oh it was just horrendous. It was the same pattern again, but just a different part of London.

So within 10 minutes of ringing up these kids' homes, (about 20 kids' homes), I pick up the phone and ask how many kids they had. They say about five.

They'll get two grand per kid. They're meant to be looking after these kids in care. These are kids that come from abuse, they're meant to get therapy and put their lives right.

But no, they get picked up at night; three of them. Three out of the five will get picked up on average and they were taken to brothels and pimped out and that was consistent of all these care homes.

So within one afternoon, I found 10. By the end of the week, I found 50. And I set up a meeting with social services, NGO's (non-governmental organisations), outreach groups, all set up for kids and the same thing happened - I was threatened. I was threatened by someone who's very high up and again, details were given over to both the National Crime Squads, the police complaints and to the government enquiry.

She's head up of one of the leading children's charities and she basically said, "you're treading on toes, you step away now. You back down now".

And then she colluded with a superintendent and basically got it all shut down.

Cooper: It's unbelievable.

Wedger: And I'll say to people, you be careful who you give money to, these charities, these leading children's charities. I'm telling you now, I'm telling you, knowing what I know now, some aren't all they seem. And that's all I can say. I don't want to get sued by them, but there's two main ones and one is always on the telly, saying "we're helping kids". You're not helping kids. They are *not* helping kids the way they should be helping kids. Absolutely appalling.

So, I get moved. Life sort of goes on to a point where, it has its toll on you. Policing takes its toll on you. It's a tough job. I was bringing up four kids. I was working as a tree surgeon at weekends to get extra money. Always on the go. But it was always in the back of my mind what was going on, what had happened. And I was thinking, this is corruption. This can't be allowed to happen. So I really wanted to speak out but I had no way of speaking out because you don't, it's just the culture you can't.

I was getting reckless because what I was doing was, I started smoking in the office and I would drink. I'd come in, drinking a can of beer in the morning. I wanted to be stopped. I was screaming out for someone to try and accost me, but no one did.

Sometimes I wouldn't even turn up for work. I wouldn't even bother. They'd ring me up and I'd say, "No, no, I'm not going in". They'd ring me up and I'd say, "No, I'm in the north, I'm not coming in" and really took the piss because I actually wanted to get arrested at the most but the very least be accosted by a senior officer so I could let him have it so I could use it as a platform to speak out.

But Jimmy Savile got exposed and I thought, wow, this is brilliant. This is it. I've got it. There were a couple of coppers that came forward. So I linked in with them and they put me in touch with politicians, so I linked in with them. They put me in touch with the press, so I spoke to the press.

I did an interview, a podcast interview with the UK Column. A lovely bloke called Brian Gerrish. He promised me he wouldn't put it out but he did. He just put it out! And it saved my life actually. He saved my life, what he did. Sounds dramatic, but it's true. It did. It definitely saved my liberty because they couldn't touch me because it was out there, otherwise they'd have nicked me.

So I made an allegation of corruption in high office and the strange thing is, this TV series Line of Duty had come out and there's a line in there and it's one of the last series all about child abuse and cover-ups in high office and someone who dealt with the professional standards for the police had given my case details to the producers of that because it is *identical* to what I exposed and there was a line in it and I know that it's been plagiarised and someone had used my case to make money working with the BBC on this drama.

And I rang up the corruption command police and said I need to speak to a high-ranked officer. They said they'd put me through to PC so and so. I said no, no, I'm not. I am not talking to a uniformed officer. No way. And I'm not talking to a man. I want a senior woman officer. In the end, they got it.

So a woman Detective Chief Inspector rung me up. She said can you come to a secure location and meet with us?

It was really weird, on my way there. I was accosted in a corridor by one of the men I was going to inform on. He was there... "How are you Jon? How you doing?"

He was part of the conspiracy to bring me down. I was thinking, what the hell's he doing there? It was really odd.

So I sort of didn't think I was really being surveilled or anything. I was later to find out, when I got my disclosure through from a civil case, that I had been under surveillance for two and a half years.

Anyway, so I went up. This woman met me and she said, "tell me something Jon. Why is it that you want to speak to a senior woman detective?" And I said, "because you cannot roll up your trouser leg". That's what the Masons do.

She just laughed. She said, "I know exactly what you mean". So over a period of days, they took my statement and then they said, "Look, you're bomb proof". But that's when the attack started.

All of a sudden, I'm being served with discipline papers. They've gone through nearly 10 years of my internet records. My emails have been trawled. They started putting me up for data protection violation, which would not only get me sacked but get me in court.

One of the whistle blowers, she told me that. She said, "listen, they're gonna have you for data protection violations. Because that's what they do to all of us. Whenever we speak out this is what they do".

So I got pulled in and they said, "right, you're gonna be sent to court and sent to a discipline panel for data protection violations, for misuse of intelligence".

I was worried. I thought, oh my God, I'm going to lose my job. So basically, I walked out and then I was done for talking to the press. I never actually spoke to the press. The story got leaked, and I ended up in the Sun, the Star. I did speak to the Express in the end but the Sun and the Star leaked a story about me.

So then I was arrested for…. "conspiracy to supply Class A drugs".

All the other cases against me were mounting up. They were really mounting up and they said they carry a two-year sentence. This one was a 15 year sentence. "We've got ya".

I went, "What you on about" and I refused to be interviewed. I refused to be interviewed and they said, "Right, well, here it is".

And what it was for, was this… my friend was an undercover officer and like most undercover officers, he went mad. Their mind goes, it's too much for them. They really ran him ragged and he had something like five different telephones, different identities and all sorts of things. And he lost the plot. Gone mad.

He left the police and went to live in France. He got lonely and he was being invited to the UK to do an interview. He had trust issues with the police but he was my mate, I was his mate. His legend was, he would live as a tramp. He'd live on the street and they'd send him all around the country and he'd just live as a tramp. He used to piss himself and he would actually smell of piss, he would stand there and piss himself because that was his legend.

Cooper: What do you mean by legend? That's his act?

Wedger: Because that was his act.

Cooper: Talk about taking the method acting to the extreme!

Wedger: Unbelievable this guy. Bearded and he used to have a bottle of methadone on him.

So I said, "you still living as a tramp?" and he replied, "yeah" and I said, "well, when you come to London, give me a call".

It was all done through the police email because my surname was so easy to find and I was on the police email system. You're going to find me easily and he did.

"So well… I'll tell you what, you bring the Tennents Super and I'll bring the methadone and we'll have a cocktail".

Cooper: Yeah. It was clearly a joke.

Wedger: Yeah. So when I found out that's what it was, I laughed. I couldn't stop laughing. They thrust the papers on me and said, "you've got to sign this". I said, "yeah, I'll sign for it. Give me a pen, because I'm going to stick this straight in your eye".

The bloke froze, he didn't know what to do. He was a Detective Inspector and he was speechless.

"Now, eff off and leave me alone. If that's all you got, leave me alone", I said.

So next thing is, I had "threats to kill", come my way.

Then, because I walked out, they stopped paying me. So I've now got no income. The bank came around to look at repossession because I can't pay my mortgage. The banks get a hard time but the woman that came round, she heard my story and she had been in a care home. She put her arms around me and said, "no one's touching your home Jon. You make a minimum payment, like £1 a month or something and the moment you're back on, we're back on with you".

So I can't knock the banks. I can't. When they say the banks do this and that, they were actually good to me. I'm not a fan of banks but this woman, bless her, she worked for NatWest bank and I'll tell you what, God bless you, wherever you are, you're a good woman. *Good* woman.

And I started then working with victims and survivors, activists. The most notable one is a man called Bill Maloney; a tough guy, a little gangster from the streets of Peckham. He lived on the street since the age of 11. A victim of horrific child abuse. My best mate, and my best mate till this day. This guy offered to give me his life savings, his money, that he saved up for his funeral, to pay my mortgage one month. All my other mates in the police… a couple stood by me, of course, but all of them *gone*. They didn't want to know. Refused to give statements, refused to back me up. Then I've got ex-gangsters saying they're with me.

Cooper: Shows you who the real mates are doesn't it?

Wedger: Unbelievable, unbelievable. I've got to give a big shout out to a lady called Tracy. She does a lot in the therapeutic community around North London, not too far from here and she did the same. I'd only known her a couple of years, and she said the same. She said, "I'm going to sell my van and my boyfriend's gonna give you money".

Cooper: How lovely is that!

Wedger: A good, *good* woman. So I was threatened with the loss of my home, children, my job. I'm now looking at losing my job because I've got to go before a discipline panel on nine cases. One of them's gonna stick, by the law of averages. One of them's gonna stick and that's it, my job's gone.

There *was* a conspiracy against me. I'd been under surveillance for two and a half years. I later found out, everywhere I was going, I was being surveilled.

I got a job on a building site, cash in hand. I was nearly 50 years old, and I'm working 10 hours a day, doing graft. I started block laying for a building firm.

Again, they go on about racism. Listen to *their* banter. You'd never get away with that in the police.

I'm out in all weathers now, with guys and one of them had been in the care system and prison and all sorts and I'm getting £8 per hour for a 10-hour day. I mean, I'm working minimum wage, hard graft.

Then I ended up in the national papers, and this guy liked me, who employed me but he said, "I've got to let you go. You've been in the papers and you're probably under surveillance".

"Don't be stupid", I replied but I *was* under surveillance. He said, "look, they'll come down on me. I don't want to but…"

So I had to leave that. Then I went and I started doing garden and tree surgery. Because I had to pay my bills. I wanted to pay the bank because they'd helped me.

Now the case is with the CPS (Crown Prosecution Service). They're taking the cases on. So not only are the internal discipline people going to sack me, the CPS are now running with the cases and they're going before a court. So I'm looking at prison. I'm looking at a Crown Court trial minimum, because I'm not accepting anything. I'm going to Crown Court and I started saying, "well, take me to court. I'll see you in court".

Cooper: And this is all… to go back to your original point… this is all because you wanted to pursue it all?

Wedger: To speak out about the cover-up around children being pimped out and those involved. I still didn't realise how deep and dark it was getting.

So what then happened, was one of my boys… and this was a pivotal moment in my life… one of my children was involved in a catastrophic and life changing accident.

I was out working, I was digging in Barnet. I was doing some digging and it was in the winter. 10 at night still digging, still digging and I go back to my car, sort of knackered, finished.

I've got 50 Missed Calls. *50* Missed Calls. What's going on? One of my children's in hospital.

Texts saying, "Please, please call". I ring up my oldest boy and he's screaming at me. He said it's one of my lads. He said he's seriously ill, he's broken his neck. He said his spine's damaged, he's broken it, he's in a coma and they've taken him to Cambridge to a specialist. I've driven all the way to Cambridge and I'm covered in mud and smoke, because we had a fire.

I get there and the surgeon comes out and said he's gone into surgery.

"We've got the best surgeon's come up from London to do it", he said.

The spinal column had been severed by 95%. It was hanging off and they held no hope for him and they said, "if we do it in under 40 minutes, he'll live, if it takes four hours, he will eventually die. Go home, get some rest".

And I can remember driving home and as I'm driving down this pitch-black road, this shooting star went straight across my car.

Wow, thank you God. Then the phone went and it was the surgeon, "It's been successful. He's gonna live".

So I went home, had a wash, went back to the hospital, and he was in intensive care for many, many months. Many months he was slipping in and out of a coma. Anyone who's ever had a child in intensive care, they call it the roller coaster. One minute you're up, they're getting better, the next minute, they'll get an infection.

So all this we're seeing on the news at the moment with COVID, about ICU's and people in comas. Listen, if you're on a ventilator, which a lot of people are on ventilators... stroke victims go on ventilators right? Spinal injury victims go on ventilators. Most of the people in ICU's, when I was in and out of there, for the best part of six months, were on ventilators. And most of them get induced comas.

So all this we're seeing in the news... ICU's are always fully booked and most of the people are on ventilators... this isn't a new thing.

So when they're going on all the time about hospitals being packed and all that, you tell me in the last forty years when they haven't been packed. You don't go into nursing to get an easy life. It's a hard life from the moment you walk in.

There's a lot of scaremongering in what's going on at the moment [COVID] and there's probably a very profound, sinister reason for a lot of that and you definitely don't collapse an economy for that either.

So a few months into it, I then go in the hospital one day, and he's there and he's been acting a bit odd, my boy. He's on all these machines and he's acting a bit strange. So I just go home, I think I'll go home and get some rest.

So I've got no money. I've literally not got a penny left. I become a blood donor because that will allow me to park in the blood donors' spot because they give me a sticker so if I put that in my windscreen then I could park in the blood donor spot and not get paid parking fines and I could also go in there and get free biscuits. That's how bad it got, you know?

I get home. I have my first beer in ages. I opened this can of beer. I always remember it was a San Miguel. I was drinking it, my phone went and it's the consultant; "Can you get back to the hospital, please? If you can bring someone, bring someone".

Well, there was no one. My kids, they were in bed and my other three were in bed and I zoomed up to the hospital. I was met by three consultants. They said, "I'm sorry, we've lost your son". "But he was alright earlier", I said. "Well, unfortunately, his organs have collapsed. His breathing has stopped. He's gone into cardiac arrest.

He was flat lined for seven and a half minutes, maybe longer by the time we got to him. We've managed to get a heartbeat back, he's on full 100% life support, there is nothing more he could be given. It's only his heart that's still going but he is probably going to be brain-dead. If we keep inflating his lungs to 100%, which we have to, we're going to destroy the alveoli in his lungs, and they'll be redundant.

So at the end of the five days, we're going to be turning the machine off. If you want to take legal representation, we can put you in touch with our legal team and get that underway".

I worked on family liaison, you gotta give it to people straight. You have to say "sorry, your son's dead". Let it hit them. So I got it and they did everything they could. Anyway so, I said, "can I stay with him". They said yeah. So I stayed with him for three days.

So I telephone someone I used to work with and said, "just to let you know, this is what's happened. I'm not playing games with the Met Police anymore. I'm not. I'm not playing stupid games. If I lose my son, I'm waging war on them. There's going to be problems. Scotland Yard will burn by the end of the day. It will burn with the Commissioner in it".

Because I was still employed by them, just they weren't paying me. So she said, "Look, I'll let them know".

I said, "tell them to stay off my back because if one of them comes around to me and I lose my son, they die. They will die".

She said ok and went and told my senior officer and the next thing, something went on there. I don't know what but it turned out they tried to discipline her, to silence her. They started attacking her.

She's made of sterner stuff this girl and she said, "you don't bully me. I've done the right thing here. You've got the wrong person. No way. I've done the right thing here".

Anyway, for three days, I just prayed... I prayed. I went in the chapel, I prayed and I prayed and I prayed. On the third day I prayed, my son woke up. He woke up and I said, "move your left foot". He did. "Move your right foot". He did. Then he gripped my hands. I just said, "I love you, son". And he murmured. He's got these pipes in his mouth. He murmured, "I love you too". We're going home son. He looked a bit confused. I knew his brain was okay. He was going to live. I've got my son back. I remember ringing my mum and said, "mum, he's gonna live. He's woke up". And my mum's crying.

I drive home. I get home and I'm exhausted. I'm worn out. I'm flat out. Running on fumes. There's nothing left in my petrol tank. I get back in. As I get back, there's two coppers.

"We're arresting you for child neglect"

And that's what they did.

The Metropolitan Police sent two officers from Hertfordshire police to come and arrest me for leaving my 15-year-old home alone... with my 26-year-old, I might add.

That's how they treated me. So that's why I put nothing past them. I have no respect for the Commissioner Cressida Dick. None, whatsoever. She is *not* serving the public. The public need to know, she's meant to be your servant. I would say remove her. She's an appalling individual. She knew about my situation and did nothing to remedy it, and was behind the sanctioning of these officers coming round [to my house].

But that's when it changed for me and no longer could they bully me. I've been hurt so bad. So the threats that went on, such as "you're gonna lose your home, your job, your children", well nearly enough, every one panned out.

I fought back. So I'd say to anyone who whistle blows, don't be frightened. You're gonna get hurt, like any battle. You're gonna get smacked on the nose. You're gonna get hurt but you must never run. You must stand and you must fight because they're the cowards. If they're doing that to you, they're the cowards. They've got a lot to lose. They're attacking.

It's a bit like the trolls. They're attacking because they've got something to lose. The good ones will back you. The good honourable ones will back you.

So that started my campaign of activism and I decided then to use the skills I'd learnt as a specialist interviewer to basically get the word out there, for the victims and survivors of abuse. So I linked in with Bill Maloney and started podcasting and then I started speaking to survivors, putting their story out, getting their story out there and then I was talking to profilers and I had Carine, the criminal profiler.

Then I thought, well, I need another professional, so I spoke to the head of mental health for the NHS, who was a guy that would be used by the Home Office to adjudicate any murder when someone claims insanity, they'd send this guy, called Ali. He did a podcast and he said, "what you're doing is important, because most of my patients have come from sexual abuse".

Then I looked into suicides, so then I'd be speaking to people that were dealing with self-harming. Then the survivors… and it was going on and on.

But then what started happening was one person would talk about the satanic ritual element. So 1 in 10 would talk about it and I didn't really want to go there. I had dealt with it in the police. I dealt with Obeah, which was a Jamaican form. It was Voodoo form but had been bastardised by the Jamaican community, and heavily used out there and I dealt with some witchcraft that had come from Voodoo.

What I found out, is that it comes from the French-speaking, African nations and witchcraft is English speaking mainly. So the Congolese were very much into indigenous belief.

And if this sounds like sweeping statements, it's not because when you consider that Benin is 70% Voodoo worship as their religious belief. A tiny country in West Africa next to Nigeria. So it's very, very big but the satanic abuse, I hadn't knowingly dealt with it.

Cooper: So at that point, what does that mean to you, that term; satanic ritual abuse?

Wedger: Well, not much and then a guy called Wilfred Wong wanted to speak to me and this guy, he's an ex-military guy from Singapore. He's a barrister, and a parliamentary lobbyist, and a committed Christian and he had spent the last thirty years investigating satanic ritual abuse, and had looked into many, many cases.

And he really has the evidence of the reality of this. So we started working together as it were and so I was using my skills, he was using his skills.

He's currently in prison, Wilfred. He was arrested on suspicion of kidnap of a child, but it looks like it's a botched rescue attempt. So it looks like he'll be in Crown Court and will fight this. This is a good man that does a lot of good.

The press did try and negatively steer him but since when were they the oracle of truth anyway. We can't trust them.

Then people started coming forward. So the moment I did an interview with him, people were coming forward and these were people that have been in care homes as well. But they were different to the other survivors. The other survivors are very traumatised or have a history of drug addiction, maybe alcoholism, a lot of anger, a lot of violence.

I started getting a lot of ex-organised criminals speaking up. Notably one of them was an ex-member of the Kray twin's firm called Chris Lambrianou, who went away for the murder of Jack-the-hat McVitie. He and his brother Tony Lambrianou.

I call Chris my uncle, we've become that close. Such a good man. He doesn't ever advocate criminality at all. The bloke's a committed Christian and what he does now he spearheads campaigns to sort of help victims and survivors of abuse that have been caught up in alcohol and drug abuse.

Cooper: Not necessarily the satanic ritual abuse stuff?

Wedger: No, not knowingly anyway, not knowingly, but he's a man of God and he understands the snares and the traps that the Devil lays for us all, because we're going down a spiritual realm now.

And then you started getting the victims of satanic abuse, and they were different because they had a thing called D.I.D (Disassociated

Identity Disorder), multiple personalities, and they would change personalities and some would even physically change.

Cooper: Wow. As a coping mechanism from the excruciating pain they've gone through?

Wedger: Yeah, it's the way that the mind works. There's a spiritual element to it as well. There's a mental element. But for instance, they'll be tortured, so part of the torture would be to drown them. So the kids will be drowned to the point of death. They want to induce death.

It's an inversion of Christianity, not an inversion of Buddhism or Atheism or Hinduism. It's an inversion of Christianity. So I have yet to deal with satanic abuse which attacks Buddhism or anything like that.

Even the African Voodoo is an attack on Christianity - the inversion of what Jesus Christ did, you know? And so, they'd want to induce death so they drown the kid. So the kid would adopt a personality to do with water.

Cooper: They're not dying though. They're near death…

Wedger: Or they would bring them back. They'd have experts in reviving kids. There was an infamous child murderer called Sidney Cooke, and that was one of his things, he'd strangle a kid and he could revive them by doing CPR and it became torture.

Cooper: Part of that torture is just for their titillation, is it?

Wedger: Yeah and also, sometimes when a kid is going through the death throes they would rape them and that would make the muscles tighter. So you know there would be anally raping a kid, while strangling them and killing them. Just sick in the head.

Cooper: There's more to it as well, with the blood as well?

Wedger: It's all to do with blood. Blood is the currency. And what I was to find out was that satanic abuse was highly structured. It's ancient, it's Babylonian. This goes back to Sumerian times. It's the worship of Baal and Moloch and Lucifer and Satan. And what I'm learning now, is Voodoo is to do with the worship of Leviathan. These are all biblical names. These are all Judeo-Christianic names. These aren't anything that is named in the Quran...

Cooper: Or Egyptian...

Wedger: Yeah, however a lot of the Egyptian text stems from the Babylonian stuff and it's well established. So it was even cited by... there was a Chief Constable called Mike Veal who was in charge of Wiltshire Police. Lovely man. About the only Chief Constable worthy to earn that title.

The people of Wiltshire, you were privileged to have a proper man, a proper man. And I mean that in every sense of the term policing you. A guy with a backbone. Not these spineless morons that we see in every other county in the UK now, and I will denigrate them because they're doing nothing to stop this. Nothing. And they need to be called out, these people.

These are public servants that are failing. Monumentally failing and no one is having the spine to speak out about it but I will. I hold no fear for these people. No fear at all.

And anyway he spoke out about it. He was attacked and rubbished, like all of us that speak out are attacked and rubbished.

Someone said to me, it was Shaun Attwood, he said to me, "you are the most controversial police whistle blower".

Because I'm the *only* one who talks about satanic abuse.

I'm not talking about drug dealing. I'm not talking about diplomats. I'm talking about satanic ritual abuse and the reality of it, and the others aren't, so damn right I get attacked, and I'm proud to be attacked.

Cooper: If you're not attacked, then you're not working hard enough I always say.

Wedger: Anyway, Mike Veal turned round and said about Ted Heath, "I'm 120% sure the man's a paedophile and a satanic abuse perpetrator.

Ted Heath's name has cropped up on a thing called the RAINS list. Now for those who don't know what the RAINS list is, it's an acronym for Ritual Abuse Information Network Support.

There was a leading psychiatrist, psychologist and therapist at the Maudsley Hospital in South East London, and she was looking into abuse survivors and she started looking at the D.I.D and she realised that those with the multiple personalities, had one thing in common; ritual abuse. So she interviewed them and she started seeing other things in common, that they were naming names. Certain names.

So if a name was mentioned more than twice, it went on the list, so there's an extended list, so it's corroborated, by a minimum of three people now. So it went on a list. 16 pages of names. There's actors. There's politicians. There was one of the senior officers on the vice unit, I was on, on there.

So I even wrote to the IOPC and said, "this needs investigating".

And I got a letter back saying, "Jon Wedger, we're not even going to entertain you. We're not even going to answer your letters". So the IOPC, they need to go to hell, the lot of them, because they are deliberately failing it.

The head of a unit that deals with child sexual abuse victims is named publicly by a professional on a list, which is yet to be denigrated and discredited. *He* is named on there! Not once has he taken it to civil court, not once has it been disputed. Yet this bloke's drawing a police pension and he's named as a satanic abuser!

So then I started really looking at "what is satanic ritual abuse"?

Cooper: This is good. Because we set up the story, the backstory. We've got a good picture of the evils that are going on, and how it trickles down into all institutions and how it goes right to the heart of the top echelons of power.

Wedger: And what I want to talk about when I return is those in power. So people that are involved in government... a group called P.I.E (Paedophile Information Exchange), and the politicians that are openly supporting this group.

And this is going to be a naming and shaming forum, but it's public domain so there's no libellous stuff here. Some are dead and they need to be spoken about, these people.

Cooper: Yeah. I mean, it's funny because if you'd have spoken about all this, even 5/10 years ago, people would have said, "you're a lunatic" but now it's all come out. For instance, Jimmy Savile was the first domino and it created that domino effect.

Wedger: God bless Jimmy Savile! That's the ultimate irony. The bloke was an active satanist, yet he did God's work. He's got no idea. It's the last thing he wanted to do.

Cooper: Yeah, not in a good way but it did manage to open things up.

Wedger: He was the catalyst. He's an evil man and I hope he rots in hell, which he is but he was a catalyst and it made it credible what victims and survivors have been saying for years and years and years.

Cooper: Absolutely. I'd love to get into that, again and go into the satanic ritual abuse stuff and yeah, if you could maybe show us how it all works.

Wedger: I will show *exactly* how it works. I'll draw it out for you. The whole hierarchy and how it operates within the government and also another element, which doesn't get mentioned and that is Voodoo, and Obeah - the African witchcraft, which is very active in the UK at present.

Cooper: And that's child related, right?

Wedger: It's devil worship, yeah. There's child sacrifice in it. There's a lot of gangsters that are involved in it. You can even go online and you can make contact with a witch doctor whose advertising services to protect you and it's all done and it will all be done from a blood ritual.

Cooper: Yeah, that's terrifying but also intriguing, because I really want to know about that and I think other people should know about that.

Wedger: No one's doing anything about it.

Cooper: No one's talking about it. It's buried. And also, I'd quite like to talk to you about Jill Dando at some point. I think she was exposing paedophilia within the BBC, I believe?

Wedger: Jill Dando... The McCanns. They're not like Jill Dando, they're wrong. They're bad.

Cooper: There's something very, very fishy going on with them.

Wedger: Awful. Appalling. And how they got away with it, I'll never know, and why the police keep throwing money at them.

Cooper: I mean, 10's of 1000's of children go missing. Why are they hyper-focusing on Madeleine McCann? There's some unanswered questions there.

Wedger: Why were the parents not arrested in the UK for the minimum of child neglect. There's child abandonment there. A clear case of child abandonment, they could have run with.

It's a knock-on effect of the McCann case, which was part of the process that collapsed the children's home case at Haute de La Garenne, in Jersey. And it's Kate McCann that had a part to play in that, in my opinion.

Everything I talk about, I want to quantify, I want to evidence. I'm not a conspiracy theorist. This is conspiracy reality. I've been at the centre of a conspiracy and conspiracy is pencilled into statute law. So if two or more people get together for the purpose of committing serious crime that's a conspiracy. Providing they're not husband and wife. So it's not nonsense.

Cooper: And that's a reality. People that just keep calling people "conspiracy theorists", need to really grow up and get it through their heads… you can't have corruption without conspiracy. You have to conspire before there's any corruption, so to say, "you are a conspiracy theorist", is just living in a fantasy world.

Wedger: Well, it's just denigrating people and I'd like to go on also how they denigrate victims and survivors with "The Bad Character Act". I think that needs mentioning. Bring that legislation into light.

And a call out to all these human rights lawyers. You should be jumping on the case of these care home survivor groups and helping them. You want to do something honourable - help them because they need help, and they need legal advice for free.

Part 2 - Satanic Ritual Abuse

Cooper: Alright guys, this is part two. This is the continuation from the last part that we did with Jon Wedger.

The first one, we talked about exposing paedophilia going all the way up to government level and beyond and this one is going to go even deeper, even darker.

This is about exposing satanic ritual abuse, so this is going to be quite a gripping episode, quite an intense episode, but one that's very intriguing and, Jon, this is something that actually ruffles a few feathers, doesn't it?

Wedger: Yeah, this is when the problems come on board. When you sort of lift that stone and you see this underbelly that has been encrusted in British society for thousands of years, you know?

Cooper: And when we hear that... I mean, I've mentioned that in the past to people and they say, "Oh, that's just absolute nonsense. That's conspiracy theory stuff" but there's so many accounts of this now isn't there, that it just can't be brushed off anymore?

Wedger: No, this is a spiritual battle. We're in a time when things are changing. People are moving away from Gods.

There's many reasons why and some of it is highly understandable. It's not en vogue, it's not trendy, to sort of have a belief system now. We're more atheistic than we've ever been. If anyone does pick up a religion, they tend to go with what's called idolatry, what suits them; a little bit of Buddha, a little bit of this, a little bit of that, and they sort of mash it into their amalgam of their own cognitive religion, that suits them. But there is a saying, that if you're spiritually lost, the devil takes ownership.

I don't need any convincing. I've seen things, I've witnessed things, I've experienced things. I've met people, I've seen people that have been in a state of spiritual torment, possession. I've had things manifest in front of me, since I've been on this journey. I don't need any convincing, and I'm not here to convince anyone either.

So someone said to me once, "I don't believe in it". I said, "I don't care. I'm not interested what you believe in. Really, not interested. That's down to you".

But the thing is, you might not believe in God, but I tell you what, the Devil believes in you, and he's out to get you. There's a battle for your soul.

What you'll find, with this path; it's very, very dark and, and the deeper you go into it, the more you understand, and then you start understanding things like, why are children abducted? Why are they killed? Why are people given lenient sentences? How can a well-known criminal know a politician? Why is it that anyone else that commits a horrific crime, gets life sentence, whereas a politician gets away with it? And then you start understanding satanic ritual abuse.

And the other thing you get with those that have been sexually abused within the home and within an institution, some of them will come out and talk. I've spoken to many, many of them and they've gone on to do podcasts about their abuse.

Satanic ritual abuse; it's very rare for people to come out and speak out but they do. It does happen. People do get to a level of healing, where they are able to, but you get a thing called mind control and that is very synonymous with satanic ritual abuse of a child. They are tortured. They are taken to the point of death and beyond sometimes and revived.

There's a lot of horrific sexual abuse. There's a lot of bestiality. There's things that their poor little minds can't comprehend. The children are used in taking part in the sacrifice of other children and babies.

Cooper: The children are?

Wedger: Yeah, I'm gonna give a couple of examples. They're electrocuted. They're drowned.

Cooper: And kept alive, some of them?

Wedger: Yeah, I mean, there's two levels here; you get children that are abducted or just born to die. They're used for the rituals and big money is traded… It's all about money and power.

Yeah, let's not get this wrong. It's about money and power. Once you understand this thing, you can understand commerce, and the CEO's… because there's a greater percentage of psychopathy in the CEO's of big industries than anywhere else in the employment world.

But a child that's born into satanic ritual abuse, is groomed and is educated in the ways of being a sex toy so they will be highly sexualised and they will know how to perform sexual acts. So there's time being invested in these children, so they're not going to kill them, because they need them and they will be used to get other children in and lure them in. There'll be used to pull other kids in; "come and play with us".

I want to go on in a minute about how the hierarchy of this goes on but one thing it does to that mind; it fragments it, it shatters that mind.

There's two trains of thought; some say that memory is stored all over the outer cortex surface area of the brain. Others say they don't know where memory is stored but one thing is for sure, it's not stored in one area because if you had a whack on the head, you'd have total amnesia. But if it is stored all over the place, then in order to action anything in life, you have to access memory.

So in order to walk and talk, you're accessing all your old memories. But if every time you did something, you were accessing extreme trauma, you wouldn't be able to move, you wouldn't be able to do anything so it gets pigeon-holed. But the thing is, it gets pigeon-holed with extreme detail. So when these memories come out, they come out with extreme detail. And that's one thing they found with trauma.

I was taught this and understood this because I ended up doing specialist interviewing skills and child abuse interviewing and became a specialist interviewer with the police and there are elements of neuro-linguistic programming in there. There's all sorts of things, all sorts of techniques have been used; psychology, and many, many things for many years and it's quite an interesting topic.

When you're dealing with survivors of extreme trauma and abuse, it is an acquired taste. You have to be properly trained before you're allowed to be let loose and to start interviewing survivors of abuse because you could easily damage them and they could go on to commit suicide.

Cooper: So they have the trauma and it kind of splinters their mind. It fragments, like a like honeycomb. It compartmentalises your mind?

Wedger: Each one will be a character. So one woman, she now helps people and she has written books on this subject. She was a victim of satanic ritual abuse herself. I've interviewed this woman. She's an incredible individual and she had something like 190 characters, and she's only a tiny little woman, very slight build. And these characters were given names. She had one character that was called Panda and I was like, "well, why Panda?"

Panda wore white and black, right? It turned out Panda was a doorman. But Panda, she told me, was left-handed, whereas she's right-handed but Panda was brought in whenever there was physical violence so whenever she was beaten senseless... and some rituals they like to beat the kids and sometimes they want to beat them and chase them through woods, which is again, another ritual.

It's Moloch. The worship of Moloch the owl because the owl will always torment its prey. It's a spiteful creature and when the owl lets it run, it will torment it, which is why it's called The Chase and people pay a lot of money to chase children through woods; catch them, whip them, beat them, and sodomise them.

Anal sex is a big thing within satanism, anal sex is and we're seeing this now with porno films, there's more of an emphasis on anal sex than there is on straight sex now.

And then sometimes kids are killed. Sometimes kids aren't strong enough and they will die from the punishment. I was told of two children that were tortured to death and raped to death by serious gangsters, and he said, their bodies are buried on an island in the UK and the guy was telling me that they were procured for a party.

Anyway, Panda was a doorman so whenever she was threatened, this thing would manifest. She said, "Panda was seven foot tall, and I was attacked once and I punched a bloke and I literally lifted him off his feet".

And honestly there's nothing of her. She's built like that pen, with a big pair of glasses, so you think my god, how's that possible?

And she went for an eye test, many years later, and something triggered her. She's got these big glasses, but she said, Panda never wore glasses, so she passed the eye test and when she signed the form, she signed it with her other hand.

Cooper: This is unbelievable. It's like becoming a superhero... like taking on a superhero alias, isn't it?

Wedger: One person I know also has multiple personalities and she will actually physically change. So one minute she could look like a boy, the next minute she looked like an East European woman, like Polish. Her hair got lighter... she changed.

It's not spooky. I'm not getting this out of context. It's not like she's a 5'5" white woman and the next moment she's a big black guy with ginger hair and broad frame.

The way I explain this, is you're about to go out for the night, right... so you'll brush your hair, you will make yourself look really tidy. You're gonna get absolutely hammered, off your face. You're sick, you get no sleep. When you wake up and you look in the mirror, the person you see hungover, tired and hurting inside, is different from the person who went out last night. You know, more so with women, with makeup and all that... but it's the same thing as when people are happy, they look radiant and so on. So it makes sense.

But they'll be given names, so one name would relate to ice because she was drowned in water. One was Sparky because she was electrocuted because they like to electrocute them.

So all these will be brought in and it will take away the memory and take away the pain. The problem is when you amalgamate the alters into one and then finally get rid of them because they're there to protect the child.

Cooper: I noticed you called them "altars", that's interesting. Like a church. Is that what the official name is for the compartmentalising of the mind – altars?

Wedger: Yeah, they're different alters. Alternative personalities.

Cooper: Oh, alters. I thought it's like altars, as in a church.

Wedger: Well, the ceremonies do take part on altars. There will be one of the personalities which will be loyal to satanism because that little child has to acquiesce to satanism because if they don't, they die, they get killed. If they resist too much, they die.

So spiritually there is then a connection so that needs a deliverance or whatever, to get rid of that. So it's a combination of two things. Now there's people who will argue with that point, but when the person wants therapy, and wants to move forward and wants to speak out, that alter will kick in and prompt suicidal tendencies.

Cooper: To stop speaking out, stop the disclosure?

Wedger: And they can't talk. So they're programmed not to talk. They just can't get it out. They'll become ill or they'll become suicidal, or they'll just become violent and kick off. But the one thing they can't prevent from doing, is drawing.

MK Ultra, or whatever you want to call it; the mind control system has never ever been able to stop someone from drawing, unless they cut their hands off or something mad like that.

So art therapy is very, very important and it's a shame because I was hoping to bring along some pictures for today, which I haven't got because the person has moved but I can bring them at a later date.

Someone who has had memory recall and put it down into artwork and it's just absolutely appalling what they're referencing. So there's a structure to satanism...

Cooper: Before we go on, you mentioned MK Ultra there. I was going to just quickly say for people that don't know what that is. That is a mind control programme and that is used in Hollywood, the music industry...

Wedger: It was post-war. Hitler had perfected it, in silencing people and controlling them throughout their lives so they don't speak out, so they do play the game.

Official documentation from the American intelligence service have been released. They've admitted that they were proactive in MK Ultra. That they've done it on various people; soldiers and all sorts and prisoners. And they have been very, very proficient at doing it. That's official.

Cooper: They're doing it now on celebrities and people in the music industry, Hollywood, right?

Wedger: Yeah, again, it's all to do with money and power. You cannot have power without a distortion, without a corruption. You can't, it's impossible.

They've shown that with the Stanford Institute when they've done these experiments, where they've just given five people power over five people without power. And it's really weird because as long as it's a uniform… in a uniform it's consistency, you know? So if you give someone a uniform, they're going to behave in a different way and if you give them power over someone else, you've got ownership over that person, to a certain degree.

Like the law gives you. Like rules in a shop give you with security guards. That person, it's going to go to their head.

And they saw it even with militia, when you've got these paramilitary groups, even having the same sunglasses was enough to constitute a uniform, and a change in behaviour.

And they found that when someone hasn't got a uniform, 1 in 13 will play up. But when they have got a uniform it's reversed, only one would have the moral backbone to say no. And that's why, when you get whistle blowers like myself, we're very, very few and far between.

As far as I'm aware, I'm the only police whistle blower who blew the whistle whilst still in post. All the others… and I'm not denigrating them, they all blew the whistle once they had retired and got their pension. So my stakes were a lot higher.

And there is a reluctance for the government to really expose this but I have got some stats with me today and I want to go through that.

So what we're looking at is this underbelly, this other world that has run parallel, so parallel with normal life, but again, it's covert, it's allegorical. So things will be hidden, in plain sight.

Before I came here, I was told to watch a video, and it was by the group The Lost Prophets and I don't know if you recall but the singer was a man called Ian Watkins. He was a boyfriend to Fearne

Cotton, so how she's never found the spine to speak out about this guy, I'll never know but he was convicted and sent away for 40 years. They still won't release fully what went on but he was sexually abusing… he was raping *babies.*

His previous girlfriend, I think before Fearne said there was no way anyone, *anyone* would have any ambiguity as to what this man was sexually interested in. She spoke out and she was attacked by social services and had her child removed. So how Fearne didn't come forward, I'll never know.

But when you listen to one of his songs, he played it and he's going on about "picking up the broken child", "picking up the shattered girl" and all this and the references to satanic abuse are absolutely in your face.

And he makes a lot of reference to the 1970's children's TV genre and he's really letting us know. This man, in my opinion, no doubt, is a survivor of satanic ritual abuse, no doubt about it.

There is a lot that this man has got to say. He's a beast, he deserves to rot in hell for what he's done but he has information that guy. I'm almost certain he has a lot of information. (Jimmy Savile had a lot of information).

You know, there was a government inquiry, which I was part of, the IICSA (independent inquiry into child sexual abuse) and they started exposing the goings-on at an apartment block of parliamentarians, called Dolphin Square and many, many people came forward and spoke out about this building and it was orgies involving young boys.

The strange thing is, a police officer got in touch with me; a retired copper and he was a security guard and he said, "I remember when I was based at Rochester Row police station", which back then had the governance, the patrol jurisdiction for Dolphin Square and he said, "a superintendent brought us all into the office one day, back in the 80's and said no one is to stop any vehicle going in or out of Dolphin Square. If they do, they will be disciplined and they will come up against me".

So he was threatening him, this guy. So who was this superintendent at the Metropolitan Police, who is he?

There's a guy that was on the vice unit, that I was on, that appeared on the RAINS list, which I mentioned before. This was a lady called Joan Coleman and when people came forward and started speaking out about abuse, it was *satanic abuse* and she wasn't prepared for it.

She listened to it and they would say names and if more than two people, so a minimum of three people had to mention a name, she'd add it to the list.

This is a 16 page document containing hundreds of names, politicians. The police officer that was in charge of the unit I was on, his name is on it.

Active satanists that were involved in the rape and the murder of children at rituals in and around New Hampshire, and the New Forest. There are actors still acting now, there are politicians that are still active now. All on that list.

Back to Dolphin Square, the police were deliberately frustrating any sort of conveyance of children in and out of that place, had they had done their job, and done security patrols to protect the politicians, because back then the IRA were very, very active, and monitored, who was coming in, they would have found taxis and chauffeur driven cars, bringing young boys into these homes to be anally raped and beaten by politicians.

Culture Club - the band from the 80's and the 90's (lead singer, Boy George), again he does what the Lost Prophets is doing and he's allegorically telling us what's going on.

There's a song called "Do you really want to hurt me". Again, what is he telling us? "Do you really want to hurt me" and when you watch the video, it's all to do with West End nightclubs, which were named in the inquiry. There's judges there. There's policemen there.

Again, the Lost Prophets video does exactly the same, showing police officers and judges involved, tied in exactly with what I was told by the children.

There were judges involved. There were police officers involved, actors involved. Money people involved. The same thing and one of the venues is the Dolphin Square leisure club, which was mentioned *again* by victims and survivors. They were taken down to the gymnasium swimming pool when they were abused and it's there. "Do you really want to hurt me?" I mean, watch it. It's telling you.

But again, no respect from people when you tell them this because they don't believe you. They call you "conspiracy theorist"… "well, that could mean this, that could mean that", they say.

I mean, the comments on the Lost Prophets video, when he says, "the broken boy"… "oh, no, that's a boy's heart broken by a girl"…

No, no, no, no, *this* is a shattered boy who's been raped and tortured. I know this but again, they won't let people like me have a say, the media have put stories out there but it's a one-off and then you don't hear from it again.

So when I started looking into this… and this is when I really got attacked and the strange thing is, that the authorities knew about this, they knew about satanic ritual abuse, and after I've done the hierarchy thing, I'd like to if we can, show the freedom of information stuff that we've gone through.

There's been, I think, in recent years, 12 convictions in Crown Courts in the UK, for child abuse that is linked to satanic ritual abuse and there have been convictions, so this isn't a fallacy.

Even in the police's child abuse training manual for child abuse officers, they make reference to the case involving satanic ritual abuse, so they do recognise it, but they don't spend enough time dealing with it.

However, what I've done with some lovely people, that have helped me along this path, is gather information from every single police force as to how many cases involving satanic abuse they've had.

Now bear in mind, there has only been 12 convictions, so we've gone back in the same sort of scale about 15 years. The Metropolitan Police is like the biggest police force in the British Empire. It's huge. It's the oldest police force in the world and they've turned around, and they said, we've had none!

Whereas Hertfordshire has had a lot. Northern Ireland, the Police service in Northern Ireland, a lot. Surrey, a lot. Hampshire... again what did I just mention about the New Forest, Hampshire, the RAINS list, all satanic abuse... None!

Again, you see the same old story from the usual offenders, all the time, "the usual suspects", as they say...The Met Police; none. It's just appalling, whereas other forces have been a lot more open with it.

So I mean, what we're pushing for is like they do with assault. You could punch someone in the face, and years ago, could punch him in the face and call them something racial, if it was linked to that, and it'd still be assault and then they brought in race hate crime. So you can't do it. It's racially aggravated or homophobic, aggravated assault or whatever criminal damage. Why can't we have that for sexual abuse? This is rape but it's satanically linked. It's ritualistically linked.

It's been very difficult exposing the upper echelons of British society; the white middle and upper classes. I've been told of so many people involved, and one of them was Mountbatten, Lord Louie Mountbatten, the Viceroy of India, the uncle to Prince Philip, that he was involved in rituals.

Ted Heath - the former prime minister, was outed by a Chief Constable, a brave man called Mike Veal, as being a satanist and attending satanic rituals. The same names pop up all the time.

We've got 600-odd MP's but we don't hear 600 names coming up, we hear the same four or five all the time. These are people that are always in positions as gatekeepers to prevent information going out and they are always instrumental in attacking those who do speak out.

So you know that saying, "they doth protest too much". Well we really need to use that sort of algorithm when we're thinking about these things.

I had a woman get in touch with me, who was a victim of satanic ritual abuse and what they do is… you can't just turn up and think to yourself, "I'm going to try Islam, I think I might pop down a mosque, or I'll go to a Sikh temple, I think I'll have a go at Sikhism"… you know, go there, meet someone, have a cup of tea, have a bit of food and turn up at some sort of ceremonial thing. It doesn't work like that. You're in with both feet.

Cooper: It's the Faustian bargain isn't it, where you give your soul away, basically.

Wedger: Yeah. Like the book Dr. Faustus isn't it, when he sells his soul.

Cooper: That's it. It's that kind of thing and they even say in rap videos, "I sold my soul to the Devil". (Jay Z). They're dropping hints through their music videos. Madonna must be some kind of absolute high priestess in all this!

Wedger: You see Baal worship all the time. It's symbolised by bull worship. If you look now at MoneySupermarket.com, that advert, there's a bull there and Baal is symbolised by the bull. So you know, in reality, it's not a bull, but it's symbolised by the bull, and you see this all the time, this Egyptian horned thing.

Cooper: I thought it was a goat's head, no?

Wedger: No, that's Baphomet.

Cooper: But aren't they all connected?

Wedger: They're all connected because they're all in the realms of Satan but like Jesus has his angels…

Cooper: …They're all fallen angels.

Wedger: Yeah, it's the antithesis. It's the inversion of it.

Cooper: Got it. Different flavours of the same thing.

Wedger: Yeah, and there'll be representing different powers. So, power, money…

Cooper: Because I've heard… tell me if this sounds far out or not, but I've heard that some of these people, they create that Faustian bargain and then they do all these types of satanic rituals and sacrifices but then from that they get fast-tracked into high positions in the music industry, Hollywood, government, let's say. They tap into this dark power, but then part of that is they have to give something back?

Wedger: Well, your soul goes. There is a trade-off. There's always a trade-off and I mean, one woman, she wrote a book, her name is Audrey Harper it's called, 'Dance with the Devil' and she was a street prostitute.

One day, as a heroin addict, someone said, "I'll give you free heroin. come with me" and took her to a ritual in Virginia Water in Surrey. (Surrey comes up a lot) and she gets taken there.

She said these people were all posh and one was very high up in the Metropolitan Police. They got a baby there and it was killed.

What I get told is, they'll get children, and they are used to kill the baby. One woman told me of five babies that were put on a table.

They'll have women that are breeders that will give birth to them and each one will represent a sacrifice for someone that's paying a huge amount of money. They gaffer-taped a letter opener to this little girl's hand and she had to then penetrate the baby in its genitals to kill it. The baby is screaming and they're making her stab it in its vagina and stomach.

Cooper: And they're all watching it and enjoying it and channelling all that towards their gods, their demons?

Wedger: Yeah, she told me once, they cut one little boy, who'd been abducted in Ireland and she said, he's still a missing child, his parents are still looking for him. She said he was abducted for a ritual and he was cut open "and I was made to bite his beating heart", she said and they will take the holy communion which would be made out of faeces, semen, urine, vaginal excretion, and vaginal blood and they'll mash it all up, and then they'll make these little hosts for them. So it's all an inversion.

We get it also with Voodoo... we're a colonial country. There are a lot of Jamaicans, West Africans that are heavy into the practice of Voodoo and Santeria, which is more like the Central and South

Americans. It's more prevalent in Spain because of their colonial past but it's still very prevalent here.

I was shown a church the other night in North London, where Santeria was practised, it's openly practised but the actual rituals will be a closed shop.

I've been shown many places, and I've been on observation in respect to satanic abuse venues but this is the first time I've gone into the African occultic system and is all the same. It's all the same... Baal worship.

Cooper: But they must be doing this to receive some kind of energy from it. It can't just be for fun.

Wedger: They do and the Devil will help his own.

Cooper: It's like a hit of something, they must get, right?

Wedger: They will move up in business. Women tell me they can have sex with any man they want. They just have to look at a man and he will want to have sex with them. They have power over men (for women). Men can have power over women.

You've got some blokes that are just absolute players, where did that come from? Well, it might be they're just charming but others may have gone through rituals. Money and power, mainly money and power. Also to get back at people.

And it's instant as well. The Devil will do it instantly. The one thing to remember is God does things because he loves you, whereas the Devil always wants something in return.

If you look at people like Beyonce and all that. Who would want their life in all honesty? Madonna, I mean, you know that you can see the darkness in her.

Once you start getting this discernment from dealing with this, there is nothing better than helping someone. Doing someone a favour. It feels good. Saving someone and helping them. It's nice. It's a lovely feeling. Yeah, money ain't gonna get you out of this.

Cooper: I actually get the feeling as though Michael Jackson was outing it all. I'll tell you why because if you look at Michael Jackson's old songs, they were all... "Smooth Criminal", "Bad", "Speed Demon", you know what I mean? And then he moved into "Heal the World", "Doesn't Matter if You're Black or White" and then his last concert, it was called "This is it". I almost feel as though there was something in that, like a second meaning, where he was about to out it and it was like... this is it, I've had enough, this needs to come out.

Wedger: And also look at the androgyny of this man. I mean, he comes across as a victim of sexual abuse. This is a black guy and all of a sudden, he's claiming to be white. I mean, really?

Lisa Marie Presley had his child and it's white. How is that Jackson's? People believed it. It shows the gullibility of the public. There is no way. I don't think he was even interested in women, to be honest.

Cooper: So you think he was a paedophile?

Wedger: Yeah. There are definite paedophilic traits in him. Yeah, without a doubt. And I say that with some qualification behind me because I was working with a profiler when I was in the police and part of his presentation was on celebrities and he used to say to me, "Michael Jackson is a paedophile". On a sexual offender profiling basis, Michael Jackson ticks the boxes.

Cooper: Because isn't it easy for the establishment to character assassinate those that are trying to out paedophiles, as calling *them* paedophiles. Isn't that a trick as well?

Wedger: Well, it will be but the fact is, if this man is a paedophile, he's a paedophile. If he's speaking out, then let him speak out.

It's like with police informants, if you work with them, they're all criminals. You don't get a police informant who's not a criminal. It doesn't happen.

You get well-meaning members of the public, who aren't happy with things but it's when criminals go, "Oh, we don't grass, we've got code of conduct". Absolute bullshit, total bullshit. Criminals grass. End of. And that is it.

I'm not here saying, "all criminals are grasses" because there's one or two that aren't but there's a lot that are and I worked in that world for many years.

This guy was a profiler and said this man [Michael Jackson] has got paedophilic traits, without a doubt.

Also, I can't say the name of this fella because he's well known in popular culture, but he is a famous footballer who's an abuse victim. Definitely. 100% an abuse victim.

Other certain things; self-harming. Tattooing is self-harming. Body piercing is self-harming. It's "I will hurt myself more than you can hurt me".

They get an adrenaline rush as well, an endorphin release. When people are hurt, they hurt or cut themselves and it takes that inner pain away. But tattooing, now it's become en vogue and become very popular but...

Cooper: Not having a tattoo is the new tattoo these days!

Wedger: Being normal and just being straight and working hard and keeping your family together. I mean, you're in a minority now, you know. This is what's happening now.

I'm not here to make a smooth ride for an adult. It is what it is. You are not going to progress in any swathe of society unless you bargain something, you negotiate and usually it is your soul.

Cooper: I was going to say then, how do we know if we are not unwittingly being drawn to the Devil. Let's say, just using an Apple Mac or something; the slavery that's involved in making the parts for your iPhone...

Wedger: You go and buy junk food, what's to say in the abattoir that there's not a ritual that has blessed that meat negatively, you know?

Cooper: Yeah, all the sigils that we use. Spelling, spells…

Wedger: Yeah, Sigils, symbols.

I want to talk about symbolism. We've got these badges printed up and it's a crocodile. This is in German – "Vonn Pädophilen Kindern" and it's to protect our children from paedophiles.

We've got them made up in every European language. The reason there's a crocodile, is because there was a therapeutic group that was dealing with kids, and again, getting them to draw because it's difficult to talk, so drawing is a powerful, powerful thing that happened to them.

And though there was a consistency throughout the world, that the children, when they drew a paedophile, they drew a crocodile, so it became the international symbol for a paedophile.

Now we see that in a very famous brand of clothing.

Cooper: Oh yeah, Lacoste.

Wedger: So it's there. Is that a coincidence or not? Who knows? But again, it's a very powerful reptilian beast, which death rolls its prey, you know, and it comes by stealth.

You've got to understand how paedophiles work. It's not a monster that grooms a child, but it is a monster who abuses a child and they're the same person.

Like I said before, the traits are similar to someone who's good at chatting up women, they know how to get to a kid. They know how to schmooze them and it's the big schmooze, that's all it is, to get a kid on board the grooming process and then *bang* once they've got them, they've got them.

But coming back to your thing about what we're unwittingly doing all the time. We are seeing it in music. I should have brought this book along. There's a book a guy called Gary Fraughen has written called "Putting a Stopper in the Bottle of Death & the Occult" and I wanted to promote it, actually.

He goes on about how in popular life, the occult is working on us; in numbers, in allegory in music, with the hertz of the music, it changed after the First World War. It went from 432 Hz to 440Hz or something like that because now they call it "the Devil's frequency".

We're looking at a lot of modern popular music. It's promoting dysfunctionality. You get people like Nicki Minaj that sing about anal sex and their like of anal sex, you know?

People like Jay Z, who openly talk about selling their soul to the Devil. Jimi Hendrix, openly spoke about it. You had the Rolling Stones tribute to the Devil. It's always been there. It's always been trendy to be like that. You had Freddie Mercury saying how he wants to go to hell. Good, because he's going there and he's gone there. You know, that wasn't a clean man.

There's a guy, I can't name him for legal reasons but he's a comedy actor. *Everyone* loves this man. The series is one of the longest going series. They love him. It's like synonymous with British life but he's wretched. He's wretched.

I'll tell you afterwards who it is. I used to like this guy, I loved his stuff. The Devil is a great deceiver. It's deception, deception, deception. That's how it works and people that have come forward and spoke out, they've been demonised and they've been put in prison. They've been rubbished. They've been accused.

Cooper: It's funny how we even use the word "demonised". That's interesting.

Wedger: It is and it's an inversion and what they said about the end times, "good will be bad and bad will be seen as good".

Back in 2003, the Criminal Justice Act brought in a thing called "bad character".

Whereas before if someone had committed offences, they couldn't use it. You could have a real prolific burglar and they couldn't say during the trial; this bloke's a prolific burglar, and it was seen as wrong. So they said, "well, actually sod this, we're going to do it. We shouldn't be loyal to these recidivist prolific offenders anymore. They want to live that way, they can cop it in a legal forum now".

They would only tell of someone's previous once they were either acquitted or convicted, and the jury were either shocked and surprised, or they were like "well done".

So they started saying, "right, we're going to bring it in now" but they didn't just bring in previous convictions. They were allowed to bring in school reports, children's homes reports…

Now, if someone comes forward after a lifetime of criminality caused by sexual abuse; robbery, violence, drug addiction, armed robbery, you know, more drug addiction, shoplifting, prostitution, whatever it might be, they're gonna get caught along the line. They're gonna get caught and they'll get convictions, usually for what they call "dishonest crime" (shoplifting) because they're paying for their drugs, right? So the word "dishonest" is synonymous with "liar".

So let's say someone's coming forward, saying that he was sexually abused when he was in a care home and a politician would turn up on special occasions, whip him and anally rape him, (which is what I've heard time and time and time again).

This bloke then, after years of torment and pain, decides to speak out, maybe against a very well-known politician or well-known actor that everyone loves. You know, a well-known singer that everyone loves… and they're straightaway going to be attacked; "this is someone who's a liar, they've got previous convictions for dishonest crime. He's a man of "dishonesty". Not only are they dishonest in their actions, but also in their words, because when they were in a kid's home, they made false allegations".

Now these kids would come forward and speak out in their naive years, that teachers are coming into their dormitory at night and touching their penis or whatever and for their efforts, they will be classed as a troublemaker, a liar, fictitious, making up false vicious allegations. And then they will be caned. Their bare buttocks will be whipped, with a small stick by a powerful man. They would then wet the bed and they will be beaten for that again, and then probably raped again for it.

So this is how it was and then it'll go in the book as; "yes, the kid did report it", so the school will be seen as complying. They were being compliant and the school's done the right thing and recorded it, but it gets twisted.

Cooper: It's hard to believe people can be that evil.

Wedger: Well, it's cognitive distortion. It's how the twisted mind works. If you've got a scam going, you will do everything to keep that scam going. If you're cheating on your missus, you will do everything to stop the truth coming out. You will start weaving a very tangled web. You ring your mate up... "Look, if my missus rings, just say I was there last night".

You're gonna do all of that. Then your mate's involved. Then this, then that and it's the same. It's just the same on a more grandiose and perverse scale and the more deceptive these people become, the worse it gets.

Now, a woman called me and she said she was involved in satanism unwittingly as a kid because she was born into a satanic family. It's intergenerational a lot of this. And she continued in it for quite a while till she managed to get out.

She suffered years and years of trauma and problems and everything else. But then she's sort of spiritually put life back and she's in a position now to talk. So she decides to talk to me. She won't go on camera. But she said you need to know how this works.

This isn't just a disorganised bunch of idiots that turn up and dance around a tombstone at night or sit there listening to an Ozzy Osbourne record backwards or whatever. This is ancient and this has structure to it and this is a business. This is a multi-million, if not billion-pound business, in the sexual abuse of children.

Deals are made and broken on this. People are promoted because of this. Politicians are put into good positions because of this and it all evolves around this. This predates Christianity and they have got powerful people, connected people, like the mafia. The mafia have to pray to a certain saint, there's a loyalty to this saint. (I can't remember the name of the saint).

They have to do a blood ritual – the mafia. These aren't clean people. Their loyalty is a demonic loyalty, and this is one of the things I've dealt with and I'm now learning how much of organised crime has had connections to the occult, in as much as armed robbers have been using the services of Juju men for protection, when they're on a bit of work, for disruption, when a case goes before the court. I'm hearing a lot of it now, a *lot* of it. I'm not saying all of them, but it's there. It's very much there.

Cooper: How would that work, though? So, let's say you get protected in court, is that because they've got someone in the court that's helping them, like the judge or are you saying this is all done in the supernatural?

Wedger: They'll do it to the spirits, in the spiritual world and they'll have their own people, right? Then you start resonating, you'll start recognising other people that were involved.

Cooper: Ok, so it's both then.

111

Wedger: It's like Masonry. How do Masons, recognise each other? Because they'll wear clothing in a certain way. They'll have those little rings on their fingers. The shaking of the hands and they'll say certain things. The police was awash with Masonry.

Cooper: Someone in the comments said, "is there a direct link between Satanism and Freemasonry then?"

Wedger: Yeah, there is. It's the same thing. There was a friend of mine that joined the Masons and he joined for benevolent reasons. His father was a Mason, and he's a businessman. He was a salesman, and he just felt like this could move him forward and all that, so he started progressing through the ranks and then he was invited to join an offshoot… a specialist lodge because they'll have their lodge and then they'll be joined into sister lodges.

If you're a bricklayer, for instance, there'll be a special bricklayer's lodge. There's a special police lodge; the lodge of St. James, which is in St. James's, in London and he ended up being asked to join the Knights Templar and so he goes along.

He said it's a really strange ritual. They brought out knives and all sorts. He had to buy a knife for it and it was in a really posh part of Hertfordshire he had to go to for it, for this ritual and he said, "they made us worship this God called Abaddon".

He said, "have you heard of it?" Anyway, I spoke with a demonologist, and I said, "who's Abaddon?" and he showed me in a book. He's one of the nine demons. He didn't know!

I mean, they say they've got the 'G' and that's God. But it's not. It's the Geometrician. The Grand Geometrician, of the universe and the Devil said, "I will be like the most high".

Cooper: That's why you have the G inside the triangle?

Wedger: It's ancient worship that they've got. It goes back to Solomon and King Solomon. He managed to harness God-given power to harness the demons. But he started mucking about and using the demons for the wrong reasons and of course, it went on to destroy him.

Cooper: So, the Freemasons, the Knights Templar. The common denominator to all of those...

Wedger: Lucifer.

Cooper: Or Satanism?

Wedger: Yeah, it's praying to all that and the Masons go under the calendar of Anno Lucis; the year of Lucifer, the year of enlightenment and this is the deception of it. The Devil comes back as the Prince of Light, but it's not light, it's darkness. The Morning Star and so on. It's benevolence but on the surface only.

Again, like I said to you, a paedophile will groom a child. It's not a monster who grooms the child but the one who abuses the kid is a monster, and that is the same person.

It's pyramid selling. That's all Masonry is and you're gonna invest a lot of time and effort into it, into learning your lines and speaking and going to these rituals and everything else. You're going to want a return, but the return is never going to happen.

Cooper: What about somebody that just goes along, thinking the Freemasons is a social club, a networking group?

Wedger: They all do, I think most of them do.

Cooper: Are they able to come out? On a low level, are they all right? Or do you think you're entangled in the web, even at that level?

Wedger: My mate came out and he spent quite a bit of time within the church, to then get discernment. He went off to get deliverance.

Cooper: Because some of my old secondary school teachers used to say they were Freemasons.

Wedger: I was in the police. I would say something like 70% of the men were Masons,

Cooper: But they were all right, weren't they?

Wedger: They were good people. Yeah.

Cooper: You probably have to go quite high up, to really tap into that dark energy, right?

Wedger: And once you're there, then that's it. Once you get right to the top, you're tuning into an energy and not knowing it. It's a bit like listening to music these days.

Cooper: I can't listen to music these days, to be honest with you!

Wedger: I can't watch telly!

Cooper: I've stopped watching telly, stopped watching movies and I can barely listen to modern music anymore!

Wedger: I'm the same. When I'm doing my building, I'll put the radio on and think oh not him and then someone will say, "watch this film" and then it'll be a film with Tom Cruise or someone like that.

Cooper: Eyes Wide Shut!

Wedger: Oh god, I can't watch it. I can't watch anything. I did watch The Passion of Christ with Mel Gibson the other day. What an amazingly powerful film, and of course, he got attacked for it.

Cooper: He calls out a lot of stuff doesn't he, ol' Mel!

Wedger: Going back to the woman who was involved in satanism, she said to me, "right, get a pen. I'm gonna make references. I'm going to show you now, how this all works".

At the bottom there's the "diamonds". And who makes a song "shine bright like a diamond"?

Cooper: Pink Floyd?

Wedger: No, it's Rihanna.

Diamonds are the term for children. On the street in the vice world, years ago, they were called "chickens". The young boys were called chickens and they had the "meat rack". But in the satanic world they're called "diamonds". It's all about procuring the diamond and again, "shine bright like a diamond", she knows what she's saying when she sings that song.

So that's what it is now. These are kids are the commodity. So bear that in mind. So what we're gonna do, we're gonna go up into a pyramid...

Now we go onto this next group; "Spotters and Lookers". Now, this is where there is a need for us to keep our society very tight and very clean. These people are sent out and they're sent out to identify diamonds.

They will watch kids that are always on the street. (We call them the "latchkey kids"- always out). They are on the lookout, *all* the time.

There was a very notorious child murderer called Sidney Cooke. That's what he would do, he would work in funfairs, fairgrounds and he would find these kids that he'd draw in, when the parents weren't paying attention and he would end up abusing and murdering them.

Cooper: Do they literally snatch them off the street?

Wedger: Yes, yes, they do.

Cooper: There's not like a long process of observing them?

Wedger: There'll be a bit of both.

This will explain it. These people could be heroin addicts. This woman Audrey, the street prostitute, she was one of these. That was her job. She was given free heroin and her job was to go out there

117

and find children. Find children for orgies and rituals and she was good at it. And they will come to her because, again, they will use women a lot because it's matriarchal. Women aren't perceived as perverts.

Let me tell you something. Let's profile a paedophile. It is not a middle-aged white man, with milk bottle glasses, who lives with his mum. It aint. This is young black geezers. These are ginger-haired people. These are young Italians, Kosovans. Every race, every religion, every age group and they are *women* as well.

When you get to satanism, you will find a lot of women involved and instrumental in the sexual abuse and the murder of children and it will outnumber men.

Cooper: And I would like to know why that is.

Wedger: You've got the Jezebel spirit. Satanists worship a thing called Leviathan. Leviathan is a God which is worshipped more by the Juju and the Santeria. It's feminine, it's serpentine, the snake, the woman and it's what's used... the cunning of the woman.

Carine Hutsebaut who's a profiler, a brilliant woman who does a lot of work with me. She's one of the FBI's top criminal profilers. She is the world's expert in profiling child murderers, and she said what has shocked her most when she did this...

"Paedophile", it's such a broad term and when you get women paedophiles, they abuse children with a viciousness that a man can't match. You will get a greater level of torture and viciousness when there's a woman involved, than when there's a man involved, and it's just how it is, she said.

So spotters are out there looking all the time, so this is important, know where your kids are. Know who you're bringing into your house.

When you've got these people with open houses, and there's always a crackhead and a smackhead coming in and there's a kid there. That kid is at risk. They're paid and they're going to be called upon. They're needed, so they're gonna make their way to the next level...

The next group up the pyramid, we've got "The Fixers".

So what was happening, especially with places like Elm Guest House, where the politicians and people of high business standing were abusing children... porno films were made. These things are always filmed.

Kids are needed for rituals, but also needed for sex parties because they like having sex with children. They enjoy it, it gets them high. There's a lot of pleasure derived from it. These are very twisted, dysfunctional people.

A "fixer" will sort it. He will organise it.

So someone's coming to town. They want to have sex with a little eight-year-old ginger-haired boy, let say. He will sort it. He will have links to all the children's homes.

The families where there's abuse going on. They all know each other. They all share their kids about with each other and so he will know, he will have his eyes and ears on the street these people and they are not resting. There's no day off for these. They're every single hour of the day looking. Not only looking but they're linking people in with people.

So when you've got a child that has been abused, it will be trafficked about and everyone will know. So if they can't find one within their gang, they *will* abduct. An abducted child gets killed. They're dead. And we've seen that with Sarah Payne. Jessica and Holly Wells. These weren't just abducted for one purpose. Ian Huntley and Moira Hindley, The Moors murderers were satanists. Mark Dutroux in Belgium, again, a satanist.

This person will be paid huge amounts of money. They may pay it down the chain. So the families may get some and everything else, there is a big money exchange. And there's a reward.

Now, what you'll find quite strange, is this word. Someone who's a fixer. Someone who will "fix it".

Cooper: Oh, yeah. Jimmy Savile. No wonder that's why his show was called "Jimmy'll Fix it". The procurer, the ultimate procurer.

Wedger: Again, it's hidden in plain sight.

Cooper: That's also the satanic element isn't it, telling you what they're doing to almost bypass spiritual karma?

Wedger: And not only that, if you are such a disbeliever... analytical people, it's got to be in an equation. They don't believe in the Bible. They don't believe in God. They believe in this atheistic analytical world and everything's got to be proven to them. Well, you know what, get on with it. Because it's your children that they'll go for, and everything else. No one's getting off this planet alive and then we're gonna go somewhere.

If you don't believe in God, that's up to you. You've been told enough times there is a God and you've been told how to behave yourself. If you choose not to, what can anyone do again? It's falling into idolatry; "I believe what I want to believe".

People were told so much that this man [Savile] was a paedophile - stay away from him. The authorities were told. Surrey police frustrated the investigation into him. He was taken in seven times by the Yorkshire constabularies over the Yorkshire Ripper case. He even had his dentures... his teeth imprints taken because there were bite marks on the prostitutes. This man was an absolute demon.

Cooper: And a necrophiliac.

Wedger: And again, birds of a feather flock together. Look at who he was connected with.

Cooper: Well, royalty, yeah?

Wedger: Yeah, and a famous boxer.

Again, I don't know the intelligence, but I'm just saying. Peter Sutcliffe too. What's going on?

Cooper: And why has he got so much money and status because all he really was, was a radio DJ.

Wedger: He was a dangerous man. He was an organised criminal, a very dangerous man. I was quite appalled by the video that Louis Theroux did. Louis is an investigative journalist, who works with the BBC.

Cooper: Well, he's meant to be [a journalist].

Wedger: How did he not know what this guy was? And the next thing you know, he's got Jimmy Savile round his house, they've become friends and then later on he says, "he's duped me".

I'm not buying it with Louis. I'm not buying it. I like Louis' interview style and all that, but there were question marks regarding Jimmy Savile and I'm not happy with that at all. So that was a damage limitation exercise in my opinion. But I mean, again, that's my opinion.

So carrying on… we've got a little diamond, that's needed. These people have gone out and done their work. They found a kid. These people have gone out and done their work, they found a kid. I'm not talking abduction, there's plenty of people that offer their kids up. The fixers arranged it…

Cooper: Why would they give their own kids up?

Wedger: Because they're perverts and there's money, and they're probably having sex with their own kids as well. So they're linking in, right? There's loads of people who do it.

Cooper: This is intense.

Wedger: This has come from the horse's mouth from someone active in satanism… "Cleaners".

This woman said, "make sure you're sat down, Jon. Make sure you're sat down".

She named a policeman and she said, "you know him, don't you?"

"Yeah", I said.

"He's a cleaner".

Cleaners are regional, so throughout the UK, a cleaner is given a certain region. She said the UK is split into five regions. So you'll get Essex, London, and Kent will be one and South Coast will be another, and all that. Cleaners are needed because there's going to be a ritual.

I've heard of places like Royal British Legions being used. I've heard of army barracks being used, Salvation Army venues being used, all out of hours. In order for that to happen, this is what I've been told…

By the way, I'm not saying that these organisations are pro-paedophile or pro-satanists. I'm not saying that. What I'm saying is, this is what has been mentioned to me and I'm sharing it with the world.

These venues get used. So lets say, we want to use this studio, at 3am, it's gonna make alarm bells ring. Literally, alarm bells ring.

You're gonna have a central station alarm, which is wired up to the police station, which is gonna get triggered.

You may have, either an in-house or a floating around security team. Right? You're going to put the lights on. People are going to turn up and park cars, it's gonna give the game away.

A cleaner is brought in so that doesn't happen. So they will frustrate any sort of effort there are for people, either unintentionally or intentionally sussing out what you're doing.

Cooper: So how are they cleaning? In what way then?

Wedger: They're cleaning in many ways, right? So afterwards, there's gonna be a lot of mess. Right? So physically, they'll organise a cleaning team so it's forensically clean. So there is no forensic footprint.

Cooper: And they're all part of it, I guess? They're still part of that group. That Mafia.

Wedger: Yeah. They're satanists, they're brought in. They're paid big money for this. They will also make sure... that's why it's important to have high-rank officers involved in this.

They're also brought in to make sure that an alarm doesn't go off. They will put dogs around the perimeter so no one breaches that wall of steel. And if they do and someone's come in, make sure they're out of the way.

So it'll be a little team out there to distract people on the outside from coming in. And that'll be their job. But also they can put DNA on the scene. They can make a scene forensically contaminated.

DNA… I'm smoking a cigarette, that fag butt, it's got my DNA that can be left on a scene and a body part can be left on the scene and things like that. (It can be deliberately frustrated).

So if someone needs to be stitched up with a murder or something, that can be easily done. So they can do both. They can make it forensically clean, or they can forensically contaminate it and make sure that no central station alarm goes off, there is no frustration, there is no interruption. And there's no comeback on these people. So very important, cleaning up and cleaning up in many, many different ways.

Now one of the things is, you're gonna need a venue, right?

One of the things I said, and this ties in with what you said about Epstein, right? Epstein's Island. When you've got a purpose-built satanic venue, you're gonna have two things. You're gonna always have cages. So kids are kept in cages. They could be portable cages or they could be purpose built or they could even be stables.

There's a short film, I think called The Coast and it's made by the drummer out the band The Stranglers. Very, very satanic. And he goes on and he's actually showing you that this guy was involved in satanism. It needs to be watched this film because he shows kids being kept in a barn, in a stable yard. Very deeply satanic.

And the other thing is a maze. Now that doesn't necessarily have to be a hedge, but some sort of labyrinth. And what was said to me this woman, "look at the aerial photographs of Epstein Island, there is a labyrinth".

Cooper: So they have mazes there?

Wedger: It might be made out of paving slabs. It might be made out of hedges. It might be made of anything, but there *will* be a labyrinth.

Cooper: What's the purpose of that?

Wedger: Because it will invoke a demon, whether it be Pan or whatever it is.

Cooper: Really, a maze does that? There's one in Hatfield house [nearby].

Wedger: Well, Hatfield house, Queen Elizabeth the 1st's house, it will be steeped in ceremonial stuff.

Cooper: That draws in that dark energy does it? So why do we use the word "amazing" (a-MAZE-ing) all the time? Makes you think doesn't it?

Wedger: Yeah, it does. Now, the next level are the "International Fixers". So these are where they'd move kids all over the world?

Cooper: So these are your Epsteins? These are your Jeffrey Epsteins and Ghislaine Maxwells?

Wedger: Yeah, that's the name that was mentioned. Epstein is an "International Fixer". That's what he was. He would make sure the kids got there.

I've been told of people saying that they were put in Hercules jets and flown out abroad. And I said, "how would a military jet be used?" They said, "because they'll have their own pilots".

It's the same with the police. There'll be police buildings that are used, but not for normal coppers. These will be for satanic purposes.

And he said, "you know, you give someone a sleeping tablet, they're going to be out for eight hours. You're not going to get many flights that go over eight hours. So it's easy to put someone out for eight hours. Easy. And then they don't know what happened".

So this is Epstein. And this is where *big* money is.

I was told about one very, very famous British singer who is an international fixer, and always proclaims his innocence but this guy said, "no, this guy is worse than Jimmy Savile".

I'll tell you afterwards his name and it will be no surprise but some people won't have it saying, "There's no way he is". But I was told he's an international fixer.

So, like Savile, they will procure children *globally*. Certain parts of the world, you're not gonna get blonde-haired, blue-eyed kids, you know? And that's what they procure.

Cooper: Aren't they also doing it to create blackmails and bribes so that you've got this person because they'll say, "look, we filmed you doing this, so then you better do what we say and put our people, our puppets in, otherwise you're in trouble".

Wedger: Everything is filmed. Porno films are made. So when the kids are procured, like I said, not just for rituals, kids are procured for parties and that'll be filmed. That might be sadistic parties.

The other thing a lot of kids say, is that when they're taken to parties, they're made to have sex with animals, such as dogs. One girl I interviewed the other day said her dad used to put some sort of pet food on her vagina, and make the cat lick it and sit there and watch while a cat licked her. Then make the dog lick her, their Jack Russell dog they had.

So, animals. It's that perversion. Animals are killed in rituals, but the blood isn't as powerful as a child's blood. It's got power. It has power and that's why they do it. So, the fixers are procuring. And who's it for?

Well, above this, the penultimate group. They're called "The Bloods". These are very ancient, wealthy families and it's all to do with blood, *all* to do with blood and blood gives a power. Power comes a money and the privilege - The Bloods.

So these are big, ancient families and they will be governing everything. They're in charge and they remain in charge - The Bloods.

Cooper: Do you have any examples? Are they families?

Wedger: Yeah, they're bloodline families.

Cooper: So it's not quite royal level. This could be governmental level?

Wedger: Yeah, it could be anything. CEO's...

But that does lead onto the ultimate group and that's what she said, the ultimate group are the Royals. And she said they are the ruling families of the world and they're all interlinked, so it's not just here, it's all around, they're all interlinked. And they're all involved in this.

I mean, I have heard of members of this family and one always keeps cropping up, always keeps cropping up, time after time.

Cooper: Prince Phillip?

Wedger: I've heard of that but it's another one. Another one. I can't say but I'll tell you afterwards. It'll be no surprise, no surprise and I was even contacted by a royalty protection officer who verified a lot; a police protection officer, so police officers, they know about this.

Cooper: But they can't do anything about it. If you look at their ancestry, they all backlink to Vlad the Impaler, don't they? And I'm sure there's some American presidents that were also connected to the Royal Family, as well. I think George Bush is.

Wedger: Let's take this down to a more local level now. This starts to answer questions. Why has this never ever got out?

Now, back in the 70's, there was a group called P.I.E. and that stands for "Paedophile Information Exchange". They were a group of pro-paedophilers who all got together and set up a working group.

So what they wanted, was the age of consent, the sexual age of consent between a man and a boy, to be less than eight years old. They had affiliations with an American group called "Eight is too late".

When their files for their membership was found, there was the head of "The Boy's Brigade", one lead person for a group called "Children Out Of Poverty". So these were charity groups, social services. There was a major in the army. There were politicians involved in this group.

These are perverted people and they had the backing of the Labour Party back in the 1970's.

Harriet Harman was backing this group. Margaret Hodge and Patricia Hewitt. All female MP's. Harriet Harman is the longest serving female MP. They're all Right Honourables, which means they are members of the Privy Council. So they're in the inner sanctum of the parliamentary world and they've got stronger connections with the Queen. Members of the Privy Council are actually physically allowed to touch the Queen.

So they're Right Honourables. There's nothing righteous or honourable about these dogs. I think it was Margaret Hodge, they made her minister for children. Minister for children?? And she is backing a pro-paedophile group that wants sex with boys at the age of seven.

Harriet Harman herself wanted the age of consent for girls to be lowered to 14. They even allowed I think, during their 1973 Christmas manifesto thing, they allowed P.I.E at the London School of Economics, to give a talk.

Cooper: It's ridiculous isn't it. They're pushing this. I can see it. They're trying to make it into part of the LGBT community – "paedosexual". That way it becomes a victim class, therefore has some kind of immunity to criticism.

Wedger: And the same with satanism, they want it to be a religion, so it has all the protection of like "antisemitism" or "islamophobia" and all that. This is what they're getting now. Why is nothing done about it?

But this group here was protected by the Met Police's Special Branch (SB), who funded them for three years.

Cooper: *Funded* them?!

Wedger: They were paying all their bills for three years. The Metropolitan Police, and Special Branch paying them for three years.

131

Files came out about paedophile politicians, was handed to Leon Brittan, who was the Home Secretary under Margaret Thatcher. The Home Secretary, for those who don't understand British politics, is the one who has governance for crime, punishment disorder and everything else. Prisons and the police, the lot. He went home and he "lost" them.

Theresa May did likewise. She lost a file of, I don't know… something like 130 cases. She "lost" them.

In charge at the time of Brittan, security services MI5 and MI6, there was a bloke in charge called Sir Peter Hayman, a convicted paedophile.

We have Patrick Rock who was the political advisor… each politician has a PA - a political adviser who basically does all the work for them. David Cameron's PA was Patrick Rock, who was a paedophile, who was caught with 25,000 indecent images of children. And *he* was in charge of internet security!

So when we sit there and scratch our heads as to how does this not get out? I'm telling you, it's ingrained. It's endemic.

We had one Chief Constable called Mike Veal, who decided he's not having this. He was a chief constable of Wiltshire and he said, "right, I'm not having this. I'm in Wiltshire, Ted Heath lived in Wiltshire. People are coming forward saying they were sexually abused by Ted Heath and taken to satanic rituals… I'm setting up an enquiry".

It was called Operation Conifer. It cost a million pounds. It totally and utterly decimated Ted Heath and his reputation. Ted Heath took us into Europe. There were rumours that he was coerced into doing that because he was an active paedophile.

I've spoken face-to-face with two victims of Ted Heath. They said he'd pick them up in his car in Hampstead Heath and have sex with them. Ted said, "it couldn't have been me because I can't drive". And the recent government enquiry, Special Branch released their files, saying that Ted Heath would drive and he didn't have a driving licence and would go out on his own. He was procuring *boys*.

So we are seeing it all the time. So Mike Veal was this guy, who's crusade was to expose paedophilia at high office in the UK. They destroyed Mike Veal. They destroyed him like they did to myself and many other whistle blowers. There was a campaign to absolutely rubbish him and trash him, which is what you get.

So the moment you speak out... you think people would come forward. Anything I said here... how is any of this about me? How is anything about me making money or me doing this for my own gain?

No, but the trolling is all about that. I do nothing but expose this abhorrence in our society, and I get attacked, so I know how it feels. When you speak out and do what's right, you get attacked. But if you were someone like Rihanna, and Jay-Z...

Cooper: They talk about absolute filth and they get loved...

Wedger: They should be locked up. They should be in prison. Because what are they doing? She's promoting the sexualisation of children. But people love them!

It's just bullshit. Absolute bullshit. But that's how the cognitive dissonance of people and the cognitive distortion of people works.

I mean, this I could spiral off, politician after politician after politician. Activity, all connected to P.I.E but also will be linked to the intelligence services, to police in Special Branch, and there is a reluctance for any of this to ever, ever get out.

Even if a politician speaks out, he is battered down and we've got members of the House of Lords. They've put the former commissioner of the Met Police, Sir Bernard Hogan-Howe, as the Lord in charge of child protection. He did nothing to stop the abuse of children and was instrumental in a campaign to take me down.

Cooper: Someone else put a comment, "How do we legally prove this is going on and who do we report all this to, if the government is so corrupt?"

Wedger: Right, the government had the IICSA – (The Independent Investigation of Child Sexual Abuse). I became a core participant, a national one, a major witness in this. My statement went in and it was authorised and it was given the green light.

Before the trial, the British government banned me from giving live evidence because they didn't want me being cross-examined. They then tried to withdraw my statement but a political argument went on at such a high level, it was allowed in but heavily, heavily doctored.

They do everything to stop it coming out and you've got to see those that are complaining, those that are being obstructive; they're the filth, they're the dirt.

What we can't do is nothing. Will I ever change anything, in what I do? No. I ain't gonna change anything. I'm only going to raise awareness. I'm not going to stop child abuse. I'm not going to stop satanic ritual abuse, but what I'm going to be is… I'm going to be a twig, a stone in their shoe, a crumb in their bed sheets. I'm going to be an irritant, a mosquito on their neck, that's what I will be. I will make it difficult for them, it will be more difficult for them to operate with impunity. It ain't going to happen anymore.

We need to raise awareness to the adults, to the children, to the school teachers, to society. We all need to take responsibility.

If you look at this lockdown that we're in now, people are happy on a very Stasi-esque way to ring up and say this person has walked their dog twice.

Yet children are getting fucked senseless, abused... yet no one picks up the phone. They say it's not their business. We hear this time and time and time again. The neglect.

Cooper: That's right. Not interested, not interested... Went for a walk during lockdown... *snitch*!

Wedger: Self-righteous cowards. It's time to stop being comfortable. Time to start calling this out because if we don't our children get hurt.

I hold no fear for these people and I am not a tough guy but I hold no fear when it comes to this. This is personal responsibility. Every one of us has got responsibility. That's why people don't want to go there. Because they just want to put on Netflix and say, "well, this isn't right. This actor hasn't been convicted..."

None of this lot from P.I.E are in prison. None of them. Whoever sanctioned P.I.E should be in prison for conspiracy to pervert the course of justice.

Cooper: How many politicians do you think are involved in paedophilia and satanic ritual abuse?

Wedger: We've got 635 politicians. We've got a lot. A few have been named, quite a few.

Cooper: I mean, Tony Blair must be right high up there. He looks like the Grinch doesn't he.

Wedger: The bloke looks racked, he looks demonised…

Cooper: He looks *absolutely* demonised. Demonised as in possession, not unfairly criticised. You only have to look at his face. He looks like the Green Goblin.

Wedger: There's two reasons he became a Catholic. One because he wants everyone to think that this is a man of God, when he's a man of the Devil but secondly, he wanted to be president of Europe. 90% of Europe are Catholic, so they're not going to accept a Protestant in charge of Europe. It's only us and Holland. We're called the Orange countries.

People, please Google this…

RAINS satanic list. It will come up, it will come up and it will show you all the names on this list. So politicians are on there.

Cooper: Wow, it's hidden in plain sight?

Wedger: It's never been discredited. It's never been withdrawn. It's never had a legal challenge against it. It's got hundreds of names of actors, actresses, politicians, police officers, MP's. My word. It's all on there. Members of the clergy. There was even the former Cardinal of the Catholic Church, Cormac Murphy O'Connor. His name is on there.

Cooper: So, can I just ask then… the whole "pizza-gate" thing. That would make sense then, wouldn't it?

Wedger: I'm not a big fan of what goes on in America because we can detach ourselves. Great Britain, we had the biggest empire in history. A very small nation. I still think that we're the tail that wags the American dog. They've got a greater stance on this and defeating it, you know, I think they've got a more open society than we have.

We've got to look at what's going on in this country and what has gone on in this country. In every children's home, we've got to look at what was going on with the BBC, in children's television in the 1970's. And we've got to demand that they're outed and any politician that stands up for them, there's a no confidence vote, they're gone. Chief Constables, if they fail to prosecute, then again, they're withdrawn.

And we've got to start demanding that we get people who are proactive in doing something because like it says in the bible, "by their deeds shall you know them". Not their words. Their words mean F all. We need people of action now. And I'm not promoting criminality in any way whatsoever but "we need doers in our movement Brian". [Monty Python quote] And we need people that are going to go out there and start doing things and if they're not going to do it, then they're withdrawn.

Cooper: How does that connect to the pizza-gate thing?

Wedger: Because I mean, what we had with pizza-gate was it was the trafficking of children.

Cooper: I think that's probably got a lot of legs. I believe it. Code words for children. If we know it's so endemic, there must be something in it...

Wedger: "Chickens" and "Diamonds". We have the same thing here; "little chickens" and "the meat rack". It's always been a trade in a kid and there always will be.

They had it with "hot dogs" and "pizza" and all that. And I mean, it's clear what's going on and how is Hillary and her husband still out and about? This is why I never put too much faith in Donald Trump. He said he was going to arrest her and drain the swamp. He didn't do it. He didn't do what he said he would.

Cooper: I'm sure they're all connected on some level? I'm sure he's part of the same gang.

Wedger: "By their deeds shall you know them". As long as they actually do something about it.

I mean, if we're going to look at politicians, let's look at Rodrigo Duterte - the President of the Philippines. Again, mixed reviews with this guy because he was going out and he had his government sanctioned with hit squads and he said, "you deal drugs in the Philippines, you die".

So they weren't wasting money on trials, they were going and shooting them and he got criticised by the Pope and by the Americans. They criticised him saying, "this man is an absolute beast".

He said something very, very profound. He did a speech, he said, "so I've been criticised by the Pope. We're a Catholic nation. We're a kind nation. Every hospital in the world is run by our staff. You've all used us. The Pope, you're a son of a whore". He called the Pope - the son of a whore!

He said, "your priests came to this beautiful island with our beautiful people and your priests had sex with our lovely children. And I was one of them". He openly admits to being sexually abused, raped by a priest. He said, "Don't you point the finger at me. I'm killing murderers. So what? You touch a child in my country, you die".

Now, I'm with him.

He said about the Americans, "Don't you dare point the finger at me, when your sailors came here, with the ninth fleet or whatever it is, you know, and you turned all our women into prostitutes, sleeping

139

with our women, and some of them were young girls, don't you come at us".

They hate that rawness, that down-to-earth working-class rawness. The political correctness and the very middle-class liberalism, that is just polluting the opinion of decent people in the UK, and we're frightened to say anything.

And I said this to the commissioner of the Metropolitan Police; Cressida Dick. And again, I would ask that the Home Secretary remove this person at once, for failing our children.

And I said to her in a meeting, and it's meant to be me and her, she was there with *nine* other women. And I think they were all from the same club. And I think these were all childless women, as well.

And I said, "I can go into a children's home, and I can pick up and groom a child. I can have sex with that child. I can get that child to get her friend involved. And I can do the same to that kid. And then me and my friends can sell them children on a daily basis, in something which is a criminal enterprise, which is endemic, and I've proved it was endemic. And you have not employed one, not *one* dedicated police officer to deal with it".

She hadn't. There was not one dedicated police officer, at that time, appointed to investigate child sexual exploitation. Not only that, she shut the unit down, the moment that I whistle blew. It was shut down and it never reopened for another seven years. *Seven* years. Disgusting.

And I said, "but if I was to lean over my fence and call my neighbour... and I said a racist word, a derogatory word towards Indians, Asians. (I don't think that way but I'm making an example here). I said you would have me arrested, you would have me, on a list or register".

Cooper: Someone recently got arrested for hugging someone on the street. Just offering a hug on the street. I mean, what is going on in the world? We're in a spiritual war.

Wedger: This is cognitive distortion, right? But you know, the strange thing is. I said, "what upsets me more than anything, is that I've just been talking about people raping young girls. Not one of you showed any emotion". And I said, "but when I said that derogatory word, someone had the audacity to have a sharp intake of breath". I said, "I can't help any of you lot and you can't help me". And that was it, the meeting was over.

And I was meant to meet with the Cardinal in charge of the Catholic Church; a bloke called Vincent Nichols, who set up a meeting with a Bishop called Paul McAleenan. When I started telling him what was going on, he turned around, and he started blaming the victims and survivors of kid's homes and how dare they tarnish the name of a good man i.e. Ted Heath.

I was just flabbergasted at this bloke's lack of spirituality and compassion. After that, I withdrew any connection to the Catholic Church. I walked outside and I said, "I'm no longer a Catholic. I want nothing to do with these people. Nothing. They're shameful. They have done absolutely F all to stop this and to have any recompense".

In order for people to get through it, they need healing and with healing comes justice. They need justice; the survivors need justice. The BBC should *not* be in operation. It should have been shut down.

141

Cooper: I just did a show about why we should be defunding the BBC.

Wedger: No one should be paying their licence fee.

Cooper: Rotten. Rotten to the core.

Wedger: My son said to me, "I haven't paid my licence fee". I said, "good, don't pay it either". You're funding paedophilia. Until they get their house in order, then they go.

Same with the police. We should be getting money back from our council tax because they're failing to protect our children. They're held unaccountable and us as people need to take an interest in this.

Cooper: So where can they go though? Did you answer that before? If someone is seeing this go on, observing it, who can they report it to, where they can trust something is going to be done, without it getting buried? Or isn't there anywhere?

Wedger: There isn't anywhere unfortunately. I'd usually say to people, go to your politician.

Cooper: Is that any good because they're probably one of them?

Wedger: Other politicians told me, "Jon it's not going to go anywhere". I've been in front of the Home Secretary's team. I've taken this 14 times into Parliament. I've been to high level. There's been an acknowledged threat to my life by a politician who said he was certain that if he didn't stand by me I'd have been killed.

The security services seem to be protecting the paedophiles and not the children. We're seeing Police Commissioners and Chief Constables that are again protecting paedophiles and not the children.

Cooper: But why? Surely one of those people would have a conscience?

Wedger: Well, they did. A guy called Mike Veal.

Cooper: That guy, ok.

Wedger: And they crushed him. I said to him, "who crushed you?" He said, "members of the House of Lords and the security services". (MI5)

We need to change this. Marc Dutroux in Belgium was outed, a million people protested. A tiny little country, but a million people took to the streets.

Cooper: I was looking at that story and he was initially let off on bail, then he reoffended, and the public were saying, "why did you let him off when you knew he had offended".

Wedger: And who were the police offers that were covering it up?

Cooper: Part of the same gang?

Wedger: Exactly. They were frustrating the search. They should be hung out to dry.

We should demand it's happening. This is what we should be doing. We should get our heads out of our own arses and all band together.

It's important podcasts like yourself are putting information out and also the paedophiles best friends are the trolls, who attack this. So any troll that goes against any of us that are speaking out about this thing, I think is dubious, and is a paedophile protector and maybe a paedophile himself.

Cooper: Those are the direct ones, but have you noticed there's the indirect ones, where they've created a culture where people are now policing each other with slur words like "conspiracy theorist". It's a way of saying, "hang on a minute, you've just said something outside the bubble, shut up because you're a lunatic if you carry on". So it makes you censor yourself; "oh I better not say that". They've socially engineered us so that people thought police each other.

Wedger: Well, if people want it, write to your politicians and tell them to get me into Parliament and give a talk.

Cooper: Maybe you should give talks in schools as well.

Wedger: The government enquiry has said I should speak to different police forces but I'm blacklisted from ever working with the Metropolitan Police ever again. They've blocked my vetting so I can't ever get a job with them. But if people want me to speak up for them, I'll happily do it but I need you to write to your politician and demand it happens. People have to take an interest. If you sit back and do nothing you are going to get robbed and society is going to crumble. It's time for us to take the power back and start making these people work for their money and earning their keep and start doing their job.

Cooper: How can we put pressure on them then?

Wedger: The first thing to do is write to them and if they don't respond then go to the ombudsman that is governing them. Again, you have to do it, you have to deal with the reasonable before you deal with the unreasonable.

We should be taking to the streets at protest to all of this. There should be positive action. We should be boycotting certain things. If there is a politician that is a paedophile, then we should all picket outside his constituency office and demand that he's removed. Or even if there's a suspicion and they're failing to account for

145

themselves properly, this is what we should be doing and it's a constitutional right to do that. These people serve us.

I say to people you should go to the Home Secretary because we take London and not one case has come out of London. I'll explain that...

So we made a request to every constabulary about how many cases involved satanism. Again, the Met Police - one of the biggest police forces in the world, they said they had none! But a tiny police like Lancashire has had 35, Hertfordshire, one of the smallest police forces in the country, with a very low crime rate has had 44. Norfolk has had 52.

Cooper: This is satanic ritual abuse?

Wedger: Satanic ritual abuse, yeah.

The police service of Northern Ireland has had 48. West Yorkshire has had 74. Yet Hampshire has had *none*! I think Hampshire failed to even reply. So did Humberside, Kent, Met Police London, Police Scotland, *all* failed to reply.

So they don't care about this. Not at all. Just blatant lies. The whole thing is just twisted and wrong.

So I was very proactive in the last couple years in what I was doing. I had a massive social media presence. I stopped all that but now I'm now incredibly active on a very, very covert level. So there's going to be more and more come out. More of the indigenous belief system; Voodoo, Juju, Obeah, witchcraft, Santeria and its prevalence in British society and how it's influencing criminality, politics and everything else.

We've already started filming venues. We've had success from day 1 with this but it's very dangerous. I'm working with a very powerful church minister, who's full-time job is deliverance; casting out the demonic. I've seen him in action and it's real and it isn't a game. People die. People don't just die from physical attacks, but from the hexes and the curses put on them. There's so much and there's going to be more as time goes on. I've got survivors of this abuse who are happy to speak out about this as well.

There is a victim of Voodoo. What she went through is an appalling time, through the sex industry. It was all set up through Voodoo to make money from her. And how much porno films are linked into this. How rife is pornography? Its inception is in the demonic. Very demonic. Pornography is the single thing that's going to punch a big hole in the moral fabric of our society. Kids can watch that with total impunity.

Part 3 - Mind-Control & Demonic Worship

Cooper: Okay everyone. Welcome to Raising the Bar with myself, John Cooper and we're back today with Jon Wedger.

This is completing the trilogy and this one's going to be even more interesting. You've got some artefacts with you, haven't you Jon?

I've actually found some things online such as in Hollywood, the music industry, celebrities talking about this sort of stuff and now I'm noticing it all. It's like now I've scratched the surface, I can see all the symbolism coming up to the surface. So, we'll talk about that for a little bit and then we have our other guest as well.

Wedger: Yeah, she is a victim of Voodoo, witchcraft, African witchcraft, and human trafficking, and how the criminal side is very linked to the occult as well and how it affected her and this is a lady who became demonically possessed and then went for a deliverance procedure. So, she's got that spiritual cleansing, but it is a spiritual battle. Her testimony is about a spiritual battle.

Cooper: Yeah so, we'll be talking to her at the end of the show. But Jon how should we tie the loop on where we finished off last time?

Wedger: Yeah, I mean last time we were going on about satanic ritual abuse and its prevalence in the UK and how it's very difficult to infiltrate. But it's the influence that it has.

I mean the RAINS list is such a powerful document in that respect. It's never been discredited. It's an acronym for Ritual Abuse Information Network Support and it's a document compiled by a very well-esteemed psychotherapist, psychiatrist at the Maudsley Hospital who would recall testimonies of people that were suffering from D.I.D (multiple personalities) which is indicative of satanic ritual abuse.

You've got to understand victimology. You've got to understand why this happens, and there's a thing called mind control and it's becoming popularly known in culture as MK Ultra. The FBI have admitted to using it and it sort of predates that.

The Nazis were involved in it as well and it's a way of really determining people's thought processes for the rest of their life and it's about understanding the mind.

If you expose a kid at a very young age to extreme trauma and we're talking extreme trauma. So these children, they have their will broken. They are submissive to their parents because there will be brutality. There will be extreme discipline. There will be sexual abuse. There will be rapes, there will be sexual abuse by the mother, so already the brain is getting very distorted and what we would deem as abhorrent for them, becomes normality.

149

I've spoken to victims of satanic abuse, that as children were made to perform oral sex on a pet dog. I spoke to one girl whose father would train the cat to lick the little girl's vagina and she was then encouraged to do it herself and in the end, that's what she would do. She would get the cat and put it down on her vagina.

Another girl was made to perform oral sex on their pet Jack Russell dog, while the adults would watch. I've heard of one lady where her father actually commissioned an engineer, a blacksmith to build a cage in which she was placed in, so she couldn't move on all fours, and dogs were brought in to have sex with her, while the whole group would watch.

Cooper: What!?

Wedger: So, can you imagine what that's doing to your mind? How that is really twisting the mind.

The children are drowning. Water is a massive element. It's really used and hopefully, our guest will allude to these water spirits that are used in demonology.

And what we're seeing is so many religions in the world and they vary. There's deity worship. Some are multiple deity worship. Some are monotheistic and some are polytheistic or whatever the word is. But satanism seems very consistent.

Whether you're looking at Santeria, in Central and South America, in the Caribbean islands or you're looking at Voodoo and dark witchcraft and then satanic abuse as we know it. Then you've got other derivatives in other parts of the world. Very similar. The demons are all the same. The demons don't change. And this is what we're looking at.

And so, different demons will be invoked and used for different reasons and they will be pleased in different ways.

So, sacrifice may be used to please a certain demon and the reward for that could be that a person wants a business deal to come off. It might be that they want promotion. It might be they want revenge.

The essence of satanism is pure selfishness, and when you look at people like Anton LaVey, what they try and do is sugarcoat it and make it very acceptable.

So, Anton LaVey started up the church of Satan in the 1960's and it started in California and they brought out the Satanic Bible and his Satanic Bible outsold the Holy Bible six to one. So, it shows people want to know about this thing, right?

And they have their manifesto. The church of Satan was like a political party and if you were to listen to this manifesto or read it, you'd think my word, this is like the perfect political party; "we're against oppression, we're against bullying, we want to work in conjunction with nature and harmony with nature". And so on.

But the main thing is, it's self-adornment, right? "Do as thou will". So, as long as you're not hurting anyone, go ahead and do it and that might sound like, well that's quite reasonable and acceptable but it's not. It isn't.

Cooper: Why is that not reasonable, in that concept alone?

Wedger: Because it sounds good, right? "Do as thou will" but you're the judge, you're the arbiter. If you've got a twisted or distorted mind, how do you know that that's not hurting someone?

It doesn't go on about empathy and compassion, none of that. It's a way of dragging people into a world of so-called benevolence. I

151

mean Freemasonry is the number one benevolent charity in the UK. Yet, you look at the arguments against Freemasonry in the fact that it's got its inception in devil worship. And there are deities such as Abaddon and Baphomet which formulate certain degrees of Masonry. So, there's enough out there on the open source about that the fact that Freemasonry is a Luciferian practice. But you talk to Freemasons or someone high up in there or someone who promotes it... I mean they supply air ambulances. I think over in the East of England, Norfolk, somewhere like that, they've provided their paramedic vehicle and they help with schooling and everything, so there's a benevolence there.

I'm not saying that all Freemasons go out there and mutilate animals and children. I'm not saying that at all but what I'm saying is you've got to look at the energy that created these things and why the need for secrecy.

Again, it's like the church of Satan, all well and good but really it's a Crowleyesque thing and when you look at Aleister Crowley, what he brought out with his Ordo Templi Orientis (OTO) which the young Geldof girl was a member of and she committed suicide. He goes on in his narrative about having sex with young boys and the sacrifice of children. The bloke was classed as the wickedest man. Yet, he's on the cover of the Sergeant Pepper album, by the Beatles.

Cooper: I was going to mention the Beatles as well. I mean their music turned didn't it? From "Love Me Do" to the LSD-based songs.

Wedger: And Ozzy Osborne wrote the song "Mr. Crowley", and you sit there and think oh, it's only entertainment but no, it's not. It's a way of slowly getting in there.

Right. If we go back to an analogy of a paedophile as we've discussed before. When a paedophile wants sex with a child, they don't just grab the child and have sex with them because they're going to get in a world of trouble and go to prison.

They've got to do a process called grooming. Now, with a paedophile, it's not a monster that grooms a child. It certainly is a monster that has sex with a child but it'll be the Romeo, it'll be the "nice uncle", the pleasant, listening ear, especially if a kid has come from trauma; "Oh, come on, I'll listen to you. Come and stay with me". *Grooming.*

That's the same as a lot of these occultic religions. It's that slow grooming process. You can't just thrust someone into these demonic environments because they're going to run and they're going to tell.

They've got to be part of the conspiracy and you get that with corruption. The reason you get these closed shops as we saw in the police, is that everyone's involved and that's why they all shut up. It's a conspiracy of silence.

With satanism, you do have this mind control element where people cannot speak out because their body is racked with a body memory and it will just bring them into a lot of agony. They will collapse, they won't be able to walk, they will get pains in their stomachs but also, there is a spiritual element to it because these children have been offered up to Lucifer, to Satan, to Baal, to many other of these demonic entities so there will be an element of possession there and that can trigger a self-destruct mechanism.

Cooper: So they've still got that element of possession within them?

Wedger: Yeah, I mean, I'm not a therapist but I have linked in with therapists and I've linked in with enough survivors and there has to be some sort of spiritual deliverance or therapy alongside trauma therapy. It's multi-level but the one thing for sure, is the damage it does is just beyond compare. They don't speak out because they *can't* speak out.

I was hoping today to produce some paintings of a victim of horrific satanic abuse because one thing they can't do... they can program the child not to talk and they do that through torture, right? But they can't program them not to draw. So, art is very important and these memories *do* come back.

Usually, they get into middle age because there is that mental stability that comes about but throughout their lives, there'll be a reason why they kept ending up in bad relationships.

Why they were always ruining, self-sabotaging relationships. Why there was a need for self-destruction, for alcohol, for drugs. Why they couldn't go to certain places. Why they kicked off with certain characters, and certain people.

They have no idea but at some point, the memories start oozing out and when it does, it's debilitating for them and there's certain triggers that might occur.

How do they silence the person? Well, you associate silence with extreme trauma and what the brain does... they have no real concept of where memory is.

Now again, I'm no expert on this matter but I did specialist interview skills with the Metropolitan Police for many years and we had to know about the psyche and it sounds obtuse but a lot of the interview skills come from neuro-linguistic programming.

There was a way in which you can manipulate people in an interview. That's why the safest bet is to say nothing. It's very clever how it's done. You can put your agenda across subconsciously to someone when you're interviewing them and they don't know.

Cooper: And get them to say things?

Wedger: Yeah, you drop it in, bit by bit, by bit, by bit and it's a clever skill, it's a very clever skill to pull it off properly, a *very* clever skill but it *is* a skill that is used. And officers were getting sent over to the U.S to do neuro-linguistic programming and this is for criminal intelligence interviewing, and suspect interviewing.

Cooper: To bring stuff out, to elicit what they want out of them or to understand them better?

Wedger: To get them to admit to stuff and to manipulate their mind.

Cooper: And to manipulate them? Ok.

Wedger: And to a lesser degree you were taught how people react to certain questions and you can see from body language, you're hitting nerves and that's where you've got to go for it.

Everyone's got a weakness and it's a matter of finding that weakness. Sometimes, it's done by being nice to someone, right? You're being nice to someone, there's a thing called reciprocity. So, if you're nice to someone, morally they owe you. So, if you've given me a cup of tea, I now owe you. I owe you a little bit of respect, a little bit of something.

Cooper: I've noticed on the streets; the Hare Krishnas will offer you a free book or something. Then try and elicit a donation.

Wedger: It's a hook to come in but what happens to these children... for example, drowning as I mentioned earlier, they would drown them to the point of death and then they will revive them.

There was an infamous child murderer called Sidney Cooke and that was his expertise, which was mouth-to-mouth resuscitation. He had revived many children.

And again, it pushes a child to death and back again and elicits an element of control in it. They will electrocute the children...

Cooper: But what exactly are they getting from that though? I don't understand.

Wedger: Trauma.

Cooper: But what do the adults get from this? Just the control or is the result to traumatise the kids for mind control purposes?

Wedger: Well, the Devil does things for more than one reason. So, sex with the child... well, why would they want to do that? Why would anyone want to have sex with, for example, a two-year-old child - sodomise a baby? Why in the name of God? It physically doesn't work anyway and the pain and the distress to the child are just unbearable.

I mean, if you left a dog outside in the cold and scratching at the door crying, it does your head and you're like oh, let that dog in for God's sake. So, how can they cope with a child screaming? Because these are twisted, perverse people.

So, not only do they enjoy it and that's a key element. (They do it because they enjoy it). Hurt people, hurt people. Now, that might offend some people but there is a factual element to that. Not all hurt people, hurt people. Out of pain comes compassion as well, so you get some of the most compassionate, beautiful people who have come from the most awful trauma because they're good people.

But when someone is hurt and damaged inside and they've not had any healing which is a key thing – healing.

Healing comes out of many things. Justice is a big element of healing and that's why our criminal justice system must be on board with this but unfortunately, it's not.

But when you're hurting inside, what will make you feel better is someone else's pain. So, if you're outside in the cold and someone's in the warm, you coerce them to come out and feel the cold with you and that makes you feel better. So, they feel better when they hurt but where does it stop?

This narcissism leads to psychopathy; "well, let's sexually hurt them, let's humiliate them" and it makes them feel better.

So, anyone that sexually abuses, humiliates, and does that, they are displaying that they are very weak and it is a weakness because strong people don't do this. They're weak and they're very much a hurt person inside and their pleasure comes from deriving pain on others.

So, the sadistic element; people like Crowley, they really emanate this in their literature and how this man was ever allowed in popular culture, I will never know. So, the pleasure will come in the sadistic element, the perverse element of defiling something that is pure, and the spiritual element because the spiritual Gods, the demigods, the demons will derive strength from defiling and shattering the spirit of that child and sodomy is the big one.

Anal sex is very prevalent in pornography now. Anal sex, even in a kabbalistic thing, it's destroying the lower chakra; the base chakra and there is a lot of research into the fact that that is a part of mind control as well.

Cooper: I've actually found a video. I don't know if you've heard of this guy, but his name is Max Spiers. I don't know if you've seen this.

Wedger: Yeah. I'm aware of Max. He died in Poland, didn't he?

Cooper: Yeah, that's right. But I've just got this here and I just thought we'd flash it up because it's exactly what you're talking about here.

[Max Spiers Talk in Warsaw 2018]

Spiers: Trauma begins in the womb of the mother and then the child is then taken away from the mother immediately and then there are a number of different ways to traumatise, to split the mind of the child so that it creates, alters. Maybe like a honeycomb, a beehive honeycomb...

Wedger: If we could just pause that for one minute. He's mentioning honeycomb. The pictures I was going to draw from... This girl calls it the hive-mind and everything is honeycombed in her mind, right? And these alters will be given names, right?

So, one of the things, she would be submersed in freezing cold water. So, her name for that alter was to do with ice but there'll be childish names because it's to protect the child. "Sparky" would come forward to protect her from the electricity.

What they do, these things when they come forward, they stop the pain, they stop the hurt but they disassociate.

The problem they have when they amalgamate the alters to make someone whole again, they will feel pain. The pain will come back. Their emotions will come back and that's difficult.

And some of these alters… a guy I know, he's got an alter; "little Jimmy" and it's the hurt child but he's reluctant to get rid of little Jimmy because little Jimmy tells him what's happening.

He said it tells him when someone's around the corner. He said it spots a paedophile a mile away and he said to me, "you're the only person, a male friend I got that I've not punched". And I went, "really?" And he said, "listen Jon, little Jimmy loves you and knows you're clean". But he said, "a wrong'un, that's why I kick off because little Jimmy knows they're wrong".

So, there's a steeper spiritual element to it as well.

There's a lady, who's a therapist called Carolyn Bramhall and she's written a book, I think it's called "Am I a Good Girl Yet", or something like that.

It's a fascinating read. She's a therapist for D.I.D. She had something like 190 alters and she managed to map them but one of her alters was called "Panda", which I mentioned before.

Carolyn is the size of that cup but when Panda was in, Panda was a door man and could knock a man out with one punch but Panda also had 20-20 vision and was left-handed where she wears these massive glasses and she's right-handed and when Panda come in once, she was going for an eye test and she came back with 20-20 vision and she signed it with her left hand.

But they know about this. So, what Max is on about, they know about.

This girl again, if I had the pictures here, it would explain so much. She draws the womb and electricity and she said she was electrocuted in the womb.

Cooper: Oh, wow. Okay.

Wedger: These are intergenerational. Children that are brought into satanism that aren't, they die.

The intergenerational kids are kept alive because they are sexualised. So, a little girl will know how to perform a blowjob, will do multiple sex acts with multiple men and it's normal [to them], and have sex with an animal, it's normal. It sounds so abhorrent, but it *is* abhorrent.

So, when we look at things like the Beatles, look at them with different eyes now. These people, their rewards were immense. Now, I'm not saying anything, because there are still members that are alive. I'm not saying they are or aren't involved because I have no proof of it but why on God's earth would you have a satanist who promotes sex with young children and the sacrifice of young boys, on your album cover.

I mean, it's like having a picture of Sidney Cooke or Marc Dutroux - the Beast of Belgium, on your book cover, you would not do it. Yet, they do. Right? So, you've got to ask why? How do these people all know each other?

Cooper: Everything you've been saying, Max says on this as well.

Wedger: I never met him but I know people who knew him.

Spiers: …Fracturing the psyche of a child which has to be done before the age of three. If it's done after the age of three, it doesn't have the same effect. So, it has to be done before the child is three years old. There are a number of different ways to do it. One of the most efficient ways, which is 99% used in fracturing the mind is electric shock treatment.

Cooper: That's literally what you just said Jon.

Spiers: This information is not new information. I think some people believe that this information was around and just began in World War II.

Wedger: Can you just pause that for a minute. Now, yeah, again, that's what I said about the war.

Cooper: Yeah, you did.

Wedger: They knew it, the intelligence services knew it. When you look at elite military training, in order to brainwash someone, you've got to break them. You've got to break them physically, mentally, and spiritually. Now, unfortunately, we're living in a two-dimensional society. People, adopt what they call idolatry. They have no spiritual substance to them because they have no need for

161

God. We all have a comfortable life. Years ago, people would roll out boats into uncharted waters, not knowing if they were going to come back.

So, they had a belief system because they needed it and if there was an omen in the sky, an albatross, they didn't go out. Anything that wasn't right, they came back. If they had a woman on the boat, they wouldn't go fishing and things like that. There was superstition because they needed it because they needed the armour of God.

We are so detached from it now and we mash our religions. The church hasn't really helped the situation with the prevalence of paedophile priests, and again anyone who hides behind the name of Jesus Christ or God in order to abuse a kid, there's a special place in hell for them. But it's taking people away from him, from God.

I've spoken to people that are desperate for some healing. They've been abused in a ritual environment, but they were abused also by priests, right? Priests abused them and then read the Bible out while they were sodomising them and then called them dirty and made them do penance after they were made to suck the priest's penis for example. So, are you going to get that person into a church to be blessed by a priest? Well, it aint going to happen.

Cooper: No, not after that.

Wedger: And this is another part of it. You can see with Max Spiers, this man is a "multiple".

Cooper: You can see he's quite lobotomised in his speech, isn't he?

Wedger: Well, he has to be. You can see that this man probably is a very tuned warrior as well. So, people will be used for many things. So, children will be used for prostitution. Some will be used for surveillance, for memory skills. But the intelligence service will use them.

Cooper: Can I play a bit more? Because I think he talks about how some are used for assassins.

Wedger: Yeah, well, you can see he's a multiple. You can see that he is.

Spiers: The reason behind fracturing the mind is so that when the mind is fractured through trauma, whether it is sexual trauma, whether it is physical trauma, or violence, the mind then fractures itself and creates an amnesiac barrier around that so that you don't have to keep reliving the experience over and over again.

Wedger: Exactly what I was going to say. Now, memory… like I started saying earlier… he's taken the words out of my mouth. They don't actually know where memory is but what they think is memory is all over the surface of the brain, a little bit like a version of the cloud technology.

So, if I get whacked in the head, if all my memory was in that exact area, I lose my memory but if you lose your memory, your memory tells your organs what to do. You've got muscle memory that tells me to do that and also, where you live and all that.

Amnesia will come in but on all levels. So, it's stored everywhere, so that doesn't happen. But what happens is, also you learn from your mistakes. So, if that cup is boiling hot and I pick it up, my memory will say don't do that, right?

And it's a healthy thing but extreme trauma isn't a healthy thing. So, if these extreme traumas were all over the mind (and this is where mind control comes in), you will be accessing them in daily life. So, that's why you see some people on the street a bit crazy and they shout and scream because they're accessing trauma all the time.

But when it's extreme trauma, you can't do it because you will collapse. So, extreme trauma gets pigeonholed, and it gets like this hive-mind thing, it gets pigeonholed, but it gets pigeonholed in extreme detail.

So, when you do access it, it is photographic, right? And that's why people when they do start getting the flashbacks, they are of such immense detail; smell, taste, touch so it's put away, and then what will happen is these things will only be accessed through trigger mechanisms. So, it could be certain words I said and things like that.

Cooper: Well, it's funny. I mean, I could just play the last part and then what I've got next... I've found where celebrities have just started in an interview and just frozen, glitched and it's just incredible. Someone's done a compilation.

Wedger: And what you'll also see explained later as well, is when people are possessed and when an alter comes in or a demon comes in and you will see them change and the main thing is, the eyes go. The eyes just go and sometimes, it might be a stare but it might be a total blackout out of the eyes which I've experienced myself, a total blackout, not in me but someone else, and also the voice will change as well. You'll get different voices.

Cooper: Why is it, have you noticed some of the people, like Ted Heath, they almost have beady eyes, black beady eyes? Do you think that's because they've possessed that dark spirit?

Wedger: It's demonic possession. People always say what a load of nonsense. Well, if it's a load of nonsense, why is it alluded to in *all* the biblical books, *all* the books of worship? In *every* single culture, it's about demonic possession and everything else. The films The Exorcist, and things like that, why are they doing that?

Cooper: Yeah, it's not from imagination.

Wedger: Of course, it isn't. It goes on.

To a lesser degree, we can all be oppressed by things. You've got intergenerational stuff; "the sins of our fathers". So, you can have an intergenerational curse, and that could be that your family are a load of alcoholics and you've got this proclivity and again, it could be learnt behaviour but sometimes if kids detached from it, like they've done with twins, they end up living these parallel lives and the same sort of abuse mechanisms. Well, how is that? Because it's subconsciously or it's spiritually programmed into them.

But we're losing our way in the western culture because we have no need for God. But you go out to the equatorial regions and these remote regions of the third world, it's alive and well and it really governs a lot and it goes into politics and Haiti is a classic example of... Haiti, the slaves have come from West Africa where Voodoo is practiced.

They've been taken over to the new world, to the slave world sent to South America and the Caribbean Islands and their slave master would not allow it. It was all done under Christianity, and they were

165

whipped and beaten if they were shown any element of their old lifestyle, so they weren't allowed to speak their own language. They weren't allowed to worship their own religion.

So, what they had to do was be very clever about this and then morph it into a veil of Christianity. So, you've got things like Santeria, they will have Judeo-Christianic saints but they will just be veils for the...

Cooper: Voodoo?

Wedger: ...Demonic saints and then you will see the same ones like the Leviathan like Baal but they will have different names. So, Leviathan will be called a thing called the "Mami Wata". And they will have different jobs. One will be to do with wealth, one will be to do with the justice system, corruption and you will see that the articles that I will display a bit later, how they are used to invoke certain demons and you can buy these things.

Cooper: God, I'm a bit worried for you to bring it out! [and show the artefacts]

Wedger: Yeah, we'll pray before we bring it out. We will pray afterwards with it.

You will see this and of course the entertainment industry it's got now a reputation for being very vile and a lot of perversions in there which we saw with Jimmy Savile.

Cooper: I'll play the end of this then what I want to do is I want to flash up where some of these celebrities have just glitched.

Spiers: ...So, after the second world war the Nazi scientists had refined the technique of how it should be done. So, what they did was, in these amnesiac barriers, they then can place triggers, symbols, colours, hand symbols, and sounds to then access...

Wedger: (There you go, the triggers)

Spiers: ...the particular alter that has been created through the trauma. So, you could theoretically create an assassin or a spy or an actor or a musician within the alters and the person whilst in the alter would have no idea that they were anything else but that.

Wedger: I mean, what is interesting is, he's going on about mind programming with assassins. Now, that goes further back. We go hundreds of years prior to that, and I can't remember exactly... it was a Turkish leader.

It was that part of the world... "assassin" comes from the word "hashashin". So, they would get killers on hashish and they would give them copious amounts and cause extreme paranoia and they would send them out to war and they would do damage.

But we see that now with child soldiers. So, we've seen it with the Biafran War. We saw it in the war in Sierra Leone, that child soldiers have always been used and they get them absolutely off their heads on cannabis, strong cannabis, and alcohol and send them to war. So, you'll get it on a chemical front, this mind-altering way and people don't know what they're doing.

I mean, I can see with Max. I can see in his behaviour, that this is a man that has come from immense trauma.

167

Cooper: This guy Max?

Wedger: Yeah. And it will be intergenerational, there will be a reason why he was used, and there will be sexual abuse in his background.

Cooper: He talks about his friend actually being an assassin... a "Super Soldier".

Spiers: ...So, a spy or an assassin that doesn't know that he is a spy or an assassin, is the ultimate spy or an assassin because he can then be questioned or asked a million times and because he is not aware that he is that, he becomes ultimately hidden. He is unaware himself what he is, so he can't be tortured or questioned.

Cooper: And then I was going to just flash this up. These are "The Swedish Twins".

Wedger: Oh, yeah. This is phenomenal. I mean what a bit of luck that this was captured on film.

[Video of "The Swedish Twins" who ran into the motorway]

TV Show Narrator: Both women run into the fast lane. One directly into the path of a car. This is turning into a serious incident.

Police Officer: Right. What we've got is, they were in the central reservation.

Police Officer 2: Why? Do we know? Do they speak English?

Police Officer: One speaks English. The one in the red. We had a block coming up because we knew they were on camera.

Police Officer 2: A full closure?

Police Officer: It's on camera. Full closure northbound. As we approached, they hadn't seen us by the way, the red one just got knocked down by the red car over there. I've got an ambulance en route for her. She seems all right but I'm not a doctor. She has been knocked down.

Police Officer 2: Is she the one that speaks English?

Police Officer: Yes

[Woman runs in front of an HGV lorry going 60mph]

Wedger: Oh yeh, she gets hit by an HGV.

[2nd woman runs in front of a car on motorway and gets knocked down]

Police Officer: We need an ambulance. Senior officers to the scene, we've got two possible fatals.

Wedger: They passed it as a fatal already, you'll notice.

Police Officer 3 Voiceover: As she ran out, my colleague tried to grab her instinctively. Luckily for him, her jacket came off or else he potentially would have been in the carriageway as well. She was obviously struck by the HGV. Once the first girl had run out, the second one for some reason also decided she was going to run out into the traffic as well.

Wedger: She goes on to kill a man as well.

Cooper: Yeah, I think… apparently, she kills someone the next day.

Wedger: Yeah. Look, she gets hit as well.

Police Officer 2 Voiceover: You can't believe that two people have just done that in front of you.

Police Officer 2: Oscar Tango 33 on arrival, both females have run out into the carriageway. The first female has been hit by an HGV in lane two, serious injury. The second female has been hit by a small vehicle in lane one. We have got two serious casualties. We're going to need air ambulances.

[Police Officer 2 tries to speak to Girl 1 who's lying on ground fully conscious]

Police Officer 2: No, come on my love, come on you've hit your head. Calm down, we are the police, we are the police, calm down.

Girl 1: No, I need a doctor.

Police Officer 2: Yeah, and the doctor is en route. It's okay, calm down.

Girl 1: I am going to fucking make sure. HELP.

Police Officer 3 Voiceover: She was unconscious initially and I mean you can see the damage to the vehicle, the windscreen and the roof as well. The majority of people don't survive collisions when they've had an impact like that.

Police Officer 3 to Girl 1: We're trying to make sure you're okay. Right, where's Paul? Oh, shit, where's Paul.

[Girl 1 gets up and runs off]

Police Officer 3 Voiceover: It was unbelievable when she started to come around and just decided that she was perfectly okay.

Cooper: She had superhuman strength.

Police Officer 3 Voiceover: Her strength was absolutely phenomenal. The only time I've dealt with people with similar strengths are those people that have been on drugs.

[Woman runs into motorway again and Police Officer 2 chases her]

Police Officer 2 to Girl 1: Stay. Stay there. Calm down, calm down, calm down, calm down, calm down, calm down, calm down.

Police Officer 2 Voiceover: She was looking to fight, she was in a fighting stance. I'm now confronted with a seriously deranged woman.

Police Officer 2 to Girl 1: Relax. Calm down. Calm down. We're police. POLICE.

Police Officer 3 Voiceover: I was joined by a member of the public who happened to be a retired police officer who offered his assistance, which was gratefully accepted. We thought we'd be able to restrain with three of us but the strength was just phenomenal.

Wedger: Yeah, it was. I'm surprised because this really opens a door to something *so* bad.

Cooper: Do you think these are alters basically?

Wedger: 100%. These are very demonised girls and what their background is, I don't know but...

Cooper: My friend said they came from an Irish brainwashing cult or something like that. I was just going to flash this up as well Jon, the celebrities...

[Britney Spears Interview – 2003]

Interviewer: That would test a lot of people's illness in the family, a breakup, this *spasm* of publicity about what happened, from Mexico to London...

Britney Spears: It was pretty rough, yeah. Yeah, it's kind of weird. Weird? Oh hello?

Cooper: It's like she's being snapped out of the programming.

Wedger: She's flipping an alter or she's going into her programming.

Britney Spears: Oh my goodness. Hel-lo? *Strong* Britney.

173

Cooper: Yeah. That's probably what the Mickey Mouse Club was about as well; MK Ultra.

Wedger: And what you'll find is, these people inter-marry. They don't outer-marry, she won't marry a plumber.

Cooper: That's maybe why she was going out with Justin Timberlake. Another Mickey Mouse Club member.

Wedger: Yeah, and again, Justin Timberlake and then she then shaves her hair off, and people follow it. So, it shows the influence these people have.

[Video of Eminem freezing]

Presenter: Starting next Saturday night, but folks I want to take you to the world premiere of one of his new videos called Berserk. Take a listen. It's headed for the top of the charts.

Presenter 2: Was that the great Rick Rubin who was helping produce that with you Marshall, when you did that?

[Eminem freezes and stares likes a robot into the distance]

Eminem: Yes, sorry, live TV freaks me out a little bit. Yes, I'm sorry, what was the question?

Wedger: Their rewards are massive, and they go on to be in places of privilege, power, and position.

Cooper: So, I'm guessing they're kind of mind-control victims probably, right?

Wedger: Well, mind controlled or that they're demonically possessed. The eyes going is a form of possession. Again, you will see it with people with D.I.D, they will change and you will actually see their face changes and someone said to me how is that capable?

And so, we'll take a woman who's going out for a night, she will be all nice and everything else and then in the morning after a night of drinking or maybe cocaine…

Cooper: Looks totally different.

Wedger: So, again, it's the same person. This will happen in your moods; you will look old and one day you will look alive but this happens very intensely and your mind's a powerful thing. These people know it.

Cooper: They know it.

Wedger: I work with a guy that was in one of the two Special Forces and he turned around and said to me that the training was so hard that when he finished, he actually thought for many years he was invincible, that he was superhuman.

Cooper: Really?

Wedger: And to many degrees, he *was* superhuman because he could do amazing physical feats but that was the programming of incredibly hard traumatic training.

Cooper: What about someone like Leonardo Da Vinci. We consider him a genius. He could draw and write at the same time. Do you think perhaps that could be some kind of mind control?

Wedger: Well, it could be and people have written books and not known what they've written; they're channeling.

You get it a lot with songwriters, they tell me, "I don't know where the song comes from, I just wrote it".

They call it "scribing", where they will channel through.

Cooper: Well, that doesn't have to be in a negative sense? You could just be channeling, tuning into your higher consciousness?

Wedger: There was a group in Norfolk and it was a group that got together and they would channel people from the past and it was to do with technology. They would channel the technology through and then they would get ideas and write them down and these things were proven to work.

Cooper: Right, okay.

Wedger: Tesla did it and he said a lot of the stuff that the inventions weren't of his thinking. He used to say that it was channelled through, came from divinity, through divine intervention.

Cooper: But is that okay or is *any* type of channeling bad?

Wedger: Well, I would have thought it was bad. To be honest you don't know what the source is. What is the source? They turn around and they say, "oh, it's this God of benevolence or this person but it's deception. The Devil is deception, deception, deception.

Cooper: You are going to the artefacts now.

Wedger: I'll go to artefacts and then our guest has got a good testimonial. Now, what I've got… these are artefacts that you can buy readily available.

Cooper: Should we do a prayer before we do this?

[Heavenly Father, we thank you this afternoon. We thank you Father Lord. We pray that as we are going to bring out all this demonic stuff, Father Lord may you protect us. Let your angels yield us and shield us, protect us oh, God from all demonic attacks in the mighty name of Jesus. Father Lord, we pronounce, and we proclaim that Father Lord let your angels stand around us, oh, God guiding us in the mighty name of Jesus]

Wedger: Amen. Thank you so much.

Right. So, what I've got… what's in here; "sigils". Sigils of the craft.

Again, we've got the pentagram and everything else and I'm going to open this in a minute and show you what's inside that and this is relevant to something I said in a previous interview with you and we've now got candles.

Now, there's a big thing about candles now and this one is very interesting, this candle, and people like them, and these things, they smell nice, they're quirky, you can buy these from these crafty shops, from these holistic shops, from these healing, well-being shops.

Cooper: You're not going to tell me candles are bad?!

Wedger: These are. Very bad. Not candles per se but *these are.* Very bad. These are there to invoke demons. These are put together under demonic possession. You can buy these, bring them into your home. You burn these, you're in a world of trouble.

So, there's quite a few and we'll go through some of them. I'll go through them quickly.

But there's… oh my word… *that* one.

It looks like a potato and again you think well that's funny. They smell nice as well which is the bizarre thing about them. One more and one more again, this is Oshun and this is Santeria.

I don't know whether I mentioned a guy called Darren Webster.

[You can watch my interview with Darren Webster on my podcast YouTube.com/@TheJohnCooperShow to watch in full]

Darren Webster was in a care home in Bath, in the West Country. He was put in there under the power of a magistrate, the magistrate ended up being a sexual abuser of him.

And his life was one of extreme violence and sexual abuse by people very high up; members of the clergy, judges, and others. One thing we don't talk about with a lot of care home abuse, is that a lot of the perpetrators are other residents and that's a result of being in an abusive environment and those that are hurt, hurt others.

Also, you've got a lot of boys that are grown up, hormonal, very sexual, a lot of testosterone, so they need to release it, right? So, there'll be access to that.

And also, those in charge, they will push it because they enjoy it. They enjoy watching boys buggering each other, beating each other and there'll be sexual violence to it.

Part of what happened to Darren was he would be put in a minibus with other boys. They knew where they were going and it's called The Chase and again, we see this program called The Chase.

Cooper: Yeah, that's right.

Wedger: We'll see these things all the time. They're taken to a wooded area, they were stripped naked, and they were told to RUN.

A group of men would be brought in. He said they were all well-spoken and he's recognised people lately. There have been links to royalty, there's been someone high up in the Anglican Church that was involved. This was all reported to the police. He made a testimony and we're talking about someone with very good memory recall on this and a man of honesty, although he had a dishonest

179

lifestyle as an armed robber. But he's in no way a protector of the paedophiles.

This is a guy that wants the truth out there and you can see the torment in this man. You can see the anger in this guy. This is a tough guy.

So, they would be stripped naked as young boys and these men would be sat around with sticks. They would run and they knew what was coming and they ran, in the pitch black, in a very ancient woodland called Rainbow Woods just outside Bath and they would inevitably be caught and this is what they call Moloch worship, right?

Cooper: Torturing?

Wedger: ...Represented as an owl because the owl will always torment its prey before killing it. You know, let it run, catch'em.

They would be whipped, they would be beaten, and they would be sodomised.

What I'm going to do now... These are two pendants. I don't even like touching these and I'm glad we prayed before this, right?

Now, it's horrible. It's got a horrible vibe through my hand as I hold that. I don't like it. This is like a man from the woods. He's represented as having antlers. You can see like a third-eye situation going on with him and the most popular name for a pub in London is The Green Man.

Cooper: That's right!

Wedger: "The Spirit of the Oak Tree". Well, look at this thing, this is what the Spirit of the Oak Tree is. People go, "oh, that's nice". They would wear them when they did the chase. This is the demon that they would invoke when they were chasing, so this is linked to Moloch and everything else. So, that is what would be worshipped when those boys were chased, whipped, and buggered in the woodlands.

Cooper: For whose purpose would that be? For the purpose of the spirit of that thing, or is it just in reverence to their demon?

Wedger: Well, all of it. They will be doing it under the praise of the demons. The demons want this.

Cooper: So, the demons get something from this?

Wedger: Yeah, because they get something from fear, right?

Cooper: Right, okay.

Wedger: So, if someone is acting as an agent for the demon...

Cooper: So, it's like a trans-dimensional food chain where they can trawl from our level. It's like food for them, on an energetic level, right?

Wedger: Of course. It's like with psychopathy. You can't reason with a psychopath and why do they do it? Because they're impelled to do it. Well, why are they impelled to do it? They don't know but again, this could be a demonic thing pushing it because a demon wants to use a human vessel to cause misery and pain.

The other thing was, it was classed as a bonding ritual. So a bit like fox hunting; it's the ultimate hunting sport, catching a kid and of course, they're not killing a fox, they are anally raping boys. Children do die in these things.

And we see this hunt a lot. We see it depicted in the paintings of survivors of satanic ritual abuse. They will paint themselves running through wooded areas.

The other one is this sigil. This is the pentagram of the five-pointed star. That's Baphomet, the horned goat and a very satanic one indeed...

Cooper: That's similar to the All Saints logo I've just noticed!

Wedger: You'll see that a lot and you see that a lot in the music industry.

Cooper: Yeah, you do.

Wedger: What I would say is, the vibe off that is bad, it's negative but...

The Ram Pentagram, the horned God as Aries appears in the vernal equinox with spring's energy and optimism. The ram pagan symbol of virility and combines with the five-pointed star connection with the life force. To energise the wearer and empower them.

The energy of this is appalling. It's horrible. I don't even like touching it. And so, these things... you bought that thing, you could be like in Camden Market...

Cooper: Yeah, you could see that.

Wedger: And in this little box, you think it's harmless, it's only a bit of metal what can it do? But in making it, a spirit will be invoked into it.

These candles, I won't go on too much about these...

Cooper: You see these in Camden Market. I am pretty sure you do.

Wedger: Yeah. They smell nice and this is about the power of love. These are demonic sigils.

But what makes this horrible is the fact that it's got a biblical Psalm, Psalm 45 on the back. So, you're reaching out then to Christian people. They think it's got love in there, this might be a benevolent thing. It's not because these are demons and when you burn that, that will release the demon into your life and things will start going wrong.

I'll just hold them up. This one is to do with court cases...

Again, links to Santeria. This has mentioned a Psalm, and Santeria is from the Christians in South America, a lot of them are linked with that and this was to get people off court cases. And this one has actually been used in a case, to get someone off a case.

I'll just mention one more, the Oshun Santeria thing, and Santeria again, it portrays itself as a benevolent religion. And they will spit rum, or it's called Aqua Diente, it's a high-alcohol drink and cigars are used. Jimmy Savile had a cigar on him.

Cigars are always used for like a smudging thing in these things and the person will be brought in, they'll be put in white and they invoke a possession.

And there are numerous amounts of Gods and one will represent water, one will represent the air or the land or whatever and the God will pick the initiate, right?

So, if you look at Harry Potter when they put the hat on someone and it picks where they should go, the house they're going in, it's very similar to that. And then it's all about being possessed, being possessed, and then offering to the Gods.

Water is used a lot. We saw a few years ago that a body was found in the Thames of a young boy called Adam. It was a decapitated torso. So, arms, legs, and heads were cut off and were thrown into the Thames.

The information I got was that this was a ritualistic thing which I think is evident but it was done for a very wealthy person to gain privilege in the business world. So, there's a high price to pay and there are only certain people that can bring them in. Do you know what I mean?

So, the path that I'm on now, is still exposing satanic ritual abuse but now, I've gone towards a part of it that is very endemic in this country because we're an ex-colony, a colonial nation, and our colonial cousins have come over here from the Commonwealth and the ex-colonies.

So, we've got a lot West Africans, we've got a lot of Caribbeans, Jamaicans and in these cultures there's a very strong belief system on the occult, which is Voodoo, which is black witchcraft, Obeah which is in Jamaica and Santeria and it is alive and well and it is Satan worship.

A victim of this was introduced to me. She was trafficked to the UK, for the sex industry. As a very young girl, she was placed under a sex ritual in Africa and she underwent this ritual which would invoke a sex demon into her.

She was brought over, placed into prostitution and pornography and in doing so, she did develop a possession and got very involved in crime but she got away, she got delivered. She's a strong Christian now and she wants to sort of highlight what's going on, expose what's going on, and encourage people, empower them to speak out.

[Interview with child trafficking & demonic possession victim Isabella. YouTube.com/@TheJohnCooperShow to watch in full]

The book I mentioned earlier called "Dance with the Devil", by a woman called Audrey Harper, she was a street prostitute and she was recruited into satanic rituals, with the lure of free heroin and told, "look, you'll get more if you turn up to this place".

This all took place in Virginia Water, in Surrey. Lots of rituals go on, all around Surrey. She turned up and she watched a baby being sacrificed and the blood was given out, she drank it and she said the moment she drank the blood, she became psychic straight away.

She said she never ever needed to be called, to tell where to turn up to another ritual, she just knew where to go and she actually took part in the sacrifice of a child. She told the police. She'd been to the police and told them.

There's another lady I know who's a therapist and she said she's killed six children, *six* children. By stabbing them. She's told the police as well.

I've spoken to about 10 people that have killed children, and they all said they drink the blood of the babies.

Cooper: This is like something out of a vampire movie. It's probably where Hollywood get the idea from.

Wedger: One woman said that the ritual is set out in churches, so they will never go to a church for deliverance afterwards. The Bible is used too...

I'm going to go on about "The 27 Club" - the book of Isaiah in the Old Testament is used. Vicars and priests are used. It's the ultimate mockery of Christ.

Different gods, different demonic realms have different values and have different genres, so for example, there'll be Leviathan which is like a serpent marine spirit, which will be for the makeup industry, for the music industry and all the vanity industries.

The Africans worship a thing called the Mami Wata - the mermaid, which is the same thing. It's the same thing, exactly the same God. Norse gods are used as well, so they're all the same wherever you go, they're the same thing, they have the same value. Poseidon, again it's the marine spirit, the marine gods and they're all demonic gods.

Even the military use their names. Military bases are used and it's a really quirky, bizarre thing because the giants, the ancient giants -

186

the Nephilim are very important to these people and that's when the great flood came to get rid of them because these were like the Gods of old – the giants, which are worshiped.

And there's a lot of megalithic sites around the UK, well around the world really but if we take the UK and Southern Ireland for example, there are many megalithic sites and they've been named to me, these places and one is in Southern Ireland and this woman said that's where she'd be taken and that's where the rituals will be and then she'd be used in the rituals; the killing of other children, babies and I'm gonna go on to talk about the babies in a minute. Sodomy is a big thing, sodomy is massive. Sex of animals is big as well, huge.

Cooper: Why though? just the perversion?

Wedger: Yeah, perversion. The gods want it and that's what they want.

Cooper: So, they're getting instructed.

Wedger: It's on many levels. It'll be for control, money, wealth, fame, whatever it is. The problem is, these megalithic sites, they're all on military land, so the military cordon off these sites, so there is no public access, so you can't get on there to dig and to find out. Salisbury Plains has got them. Again, the Irish Army have got one in Donegal and they've all been named to me and again they all appear...

I spoke with one woman, she was a street prostitute and she would be offered £2000 to get pregnant and have a child and she would go to a place in Brompton, in West London to give birth to the child.

She said sometimes it'd be in Brompton Cemetery itself. She'd actually give birth in there and the child will just go straight away, be taken. She'd get £2000 cash given to her.

Sometimes if there were complications, there'd be a doctor that they would use and she said there was quite a few girls doing it.

I've even got her transcript. It gets reported it doesn't go anywhere. These things do get reported and they don't go anywhere. So anyway, that's how they get hold of babies. They get them from the street prostitutes and things like that.

As I said, Audrey Harper wrote a book and she went to the police. It's so well documented in her book and I've heard account after account after account.

The holy bread will be made out of faeces, menstrual blood and semen and they would mash it up and bake it into a bread and eat that. Defecation is used, urination…

Cooper: Yeah, they eat shit don't they?

Wedger: One guy told me his parents are satanists, he was involved in satanism, and he said that every single big celebrity has eaten shit.

Cooper: To get to that level, they're probably going through some kind of ritual, maybe not the killing stuff but on some kind of level of ritual, right?

Wedger: I was told, you do not attend a ritual without drinking the blood, it's impossible.

There's a copper who speaks... and again I've got to be careful what to say here... and he reckons he stumbled on a ritual and made out he was passing by and whatever. It's a lie. There's no spectators in this game, it's too dangerous for them, the risks are too high. You're in it both feet and you ain't getting out, you ain't getting out.

As I keep saying, if anyone wants to check the validity of this, read the RAINS list - a 16 page document of the who's who of satanism, in the UK.

One of my old bosses from the Met Police is named on it. Again, I gave it to the department that deals with corruption and it went to the Home Secretary and it was eventually handed to Theresa May.

One woman who was a prostitute told me she was approached by this same copper and was told, "if you're pregnant, you can come and see our people".

Homeless people would be killed in these rituals but this girl said there was, on an altar, three little babies and they got a letter opener and gaffer taped it around her hand and she had a pure white gown on and she had to repeatedly stab each one in the vagina to kill them and then with the blood she said women came down naked and they smeared the blood all over themselves and then performed oral sex and then an orgy took part with everyone.

I heard a ritual took place and that was a footballer wanting to get into the Premier League… a ritual was done.

Cooper: What? Are you saying that it gives them like a power or something?

Wedger: Yeah. I heard of a famous boxer as well, who got so deep into the occult, to get somewhere, he had to go to Christianity because he couldn't see a way out. He was going mad and he became a very staunch Christian.

I've heard it all. The same venues… The New Forest is used a lot, in Hampshire. Hampshire seems to be a hotbed for it…

Cooper: Didn't you say in these rituals, it's like the movie Eyes Wide Shut, where they're wearing the robes and stuff and is there not a release of some kind of energy in the room, through the killing of the purity of the child. Isn't there some kind of release, an energetic cascading out to everyone in the room?

Wedger: It's all ritualistic. So, one woman said that they got a little child and she was made to cut the baby's throat and they usually cut the throat and then they slice it down the middle like a cross. Again, mimicking Jesus Christ.

They got a little baby lamb and they cut it open and the guts all fell on her and they said, "that's the Lamb of God". And they would say to them, "where is your God, where is Jesus now, where is your God?" So they would never go and get a deliverance to help them.

Honestly, I've never ever heard an account where it's against any other religion than Christianity.

So one girl said she didn't want to cut this baby's throat. She didn't want to because she had a heart you know. She was six years old, so she deliberately cut it different so it wouldn't die, so what they did was they punished her by sodomising her and putting a hot poker in her anus.

She told me on another occasion when there was a young boy that was killed. He went down as a "missper". He's still an official missing person. I mentioned this boy before to you.

We did supply the information, this was in Ireland and she said he's not missing, he was killed in a ritual and she gave all the information about it and she said they cut his throat and the moment he died and he collapsed, she said it was like a wave of electricity went across the room and as they were all around, it hit them concentrically like that, and she said there were these gasps and they all started squealing like pigs going "wheeee". Like pigs.

As this wave of energy hit them, she said the moment the kid gets killed because the demon's appeased.

Cooper: But are the attendees actually enjoying it? They got a hit from that?

Wedger: Yeah and every kid or animal that's killed, there'll be a price paid for that so they'll pay £2000 pounds to get the kid, you know off the prostitute or whoever and they'll have their own women that will get pregnant and bring these children in, and they're called "Breeders" but every time, every time this is done, someone would have paid a lot of money for a business deal.

There was quite a well-known guy called Ronald Bernard who was a banker for a big European bank and he actually gives a testimony. Google him. It's about how he got into merchant banking.

He's doing well and then he was approached by people saying you can take this to another level and he went to a party and he said it was just a big posh piss up but then it turned into an orgy and he was introduced to a higher level of banking with bigger rewards and he ended up entering into that but then it started going into children. Children were being brought in and he says that at that point, he said no.

He knew that after the orgy, the children were killed, which ties in with so much of what we hear anyway and he gives his testimony and he came to see me and he said, "I'm the enemy" because he didn't say he ever got involved, he said he actually stopped because he was abused as a child and he saw it was abhorrent.

I have to take his word for that you know. I'm not making any judgment either way.

My Lord, my saviour was Jesus Christ, he's my protector and I suggest that no one looks into this unless they have protection because it's spiritual. You dive into this world, you've got no spiritual protection, if you don't believe in it, well good luck with that one, good luck with that one because accounts of spiritual presence and everything else, it goes back to the beginning of time, so anyone who thinks they know better, well good luck with that.

I'm not here to punch Christianity down anyone's throat but I'm telling you now, I would not look into any of this without the protection backing of Jesus Christ. I wouldn't even go near it and even talking about it, I pray for our protection but it needs exposing and God wants it exposed and it's very real. We are going to see it, coming out.

Cooper: How prevalent is this, do you think? It's probably a lot more than we think…

Wedger: If satanists say they don't do it, well then let people come and film your rituals then. When you have a satanic ritual, open your doors but they won't, they won't do it.

There was a woman who was abused as a child and her parents are satanists and she escaped a ritual. She actually ran out naked and she was found and she ended up in the care system and she was protected.

She went on to become a barrister and she even got herself a job teaching detectives; a detective training school for police and she had an input on a course, at a residency and she used to say, "if you ever go to a crime scene, in any place of worship, think SRA".

Funnily enough, a senior copper shut her down and it's the same name that keeps cropping up, the same copper, the same guy, the same one who claims to have walked past a satanic ritual and got caught there.

Lo and behold, he's the same one who stopped this woman. He was at meeting this guy and I walked in with Bill Maloney. He climbed over a row of chairs and ran out the door. He wouldn't even talk to me, he was gone like a bullet, woosh, straight out the door.

Let's get on to this 27 Club, right? Jim Morrison, Amy Winehouse, and all that. Now, I don't know these people's personal lives. I have no idea what went on but if we look at what we're talking about; fame, fortune… and the Devil is the Prince of the World. The way it says in the Bible, the Devil *was* the Prince of the World. We are living in the Devil's domain.

God created it but if a third of the angels fell and if Lucifer convinced them to follow him, convinced them… you're talking about highly evolved, highly intelligent angelic beings, cleverer than us. Then for the Devil to deceive us, is nothing. It's easy, it's child's play, right? And a third is powerful. It's a lot, it's a hell of a lot. So, we're up against a big enemy.

So, the book of Isaiah rebukes the Devil. The Devil says in it, "I will ascend above the clouds, I will ascend to the heavens, I will be above the most high". Never actually been the most high but it'll be a replication of the most high.

The book of Isaiah is a mini-Bible. It rebukes the Devil because he wants to be like the most high.

So, they use that in the satanic rituals; the Bible is used in it, and the book of Psalms is used in it because it has power, all holds power. Everything is an inversion, basically.

Now, when someone is born into satanism, they're born into chaos and pain. So, there'll be a need to disrupt the birth to make the birth laboured and traumatic.

So, these people that say it's benevolent, there's nothing benevolent about it. It really is a lie. It's very twisted.

194

Cooper: Yeah, it is like the electric shock treatment we mentioned before, or something like that?

Wedger: All sorts. So, this one guy said when he was born, this priest came along and the priest had inserted a small pencil into his anus to cause trauma to his anus. And, of course, he's given up to Satan from the birth.

The kids will then have to go through this whole satanic ritualistic lifestyle which involves perversion. Sodomy is a big thing.

He goes on to give many accounts. It's probably the most intense meeting I've ever had with someone. It was an eight-hour interview with this guy and it was very traumatic. Myself and another guy had to spend quite a long time in prayer in a church afterwards. We were in big trouble, very big trouble after meeting this guy. Some very strange stuff started happening. And so, I've learned a lot from that.

Anyway, he corroborated a lot about the RAINS list and a lot of other stuff that I know. But he said you get to the age of reasoning, which is 13. (Numbers are very important to the demonic), very important. That's why dates are used and it has to be on that date.

So, he said just before your birthday, you would have gone through trauma, and they'll use words to invoke silence and acquiescence and compliance.

He gave me this code word and it's two words, and when you research them, one is the river that flows through Hades. It's not the River Styx, it's something else. When you cross over, you forget your life and you go into a new life. The other one was the Norse god that was blind. So that then he's blind and so he forgets everything.

So, this is said to him, he's totally amnesiac and he doesn't see what's going on and he's then sodomised and he said sodomy really is the key. It always involves sodomy and it's quite funny, not funny but ironic, because Winston Churchill had a saying that "all good evenings end in sodomy". Very bizarre. We've got to look at these people.

And then he would just be frozen this guy and then he would be in a ritual but he'll be a participant in this ritual, an active participant and this is the first time where he now takes control and a kid's killed.

He had to be careful what he told me because he's admitting now to something that could get him in a lot of trouble. And then he's left alone for 13 years. Well, where does that take us up to? What age? **26.**

Now, what happens to people, they get to this age and they start thinking this is wrong. No money and no fame is worth this and when you look at people, look how they go downhill. Look at how Amy Winehouse went downhill.

I'm not saying she was involved in this but I'm saying it could explain a lot. This wasn't good what happened to her. That was a beautiful girl with a beautiful voice and then they pushed this drug addict in her way, this Blake character and then she looked like one of the whores that I dealt with on the street.

He said, what happens is that they won't take part in the second "I will" and so, there are these four "I will's" and the last one is "I will be like the most high", three more 13 years down the line. So, they've got you in total servitude throughout your life.

Between the two thirteen years, you'll carry on. He said you could even go to church. You'll even live a normal life but every now and then a ritual might occur or whatever and you'll have amnesia brought in and what will happen is on your next birthday, the 26th, you are going to be taking part in that second "I will" and people say no. Well, you can't opt out of this.

So, you say no at 26, next year you're dead.

Cooper: There's a price to pay.

Wedger: Yeah, and that's why the "27 Club". Now, who knows if it's true or not but doesn't it make sense?

Cooper: Yeah. I mean there are a lot of artists that probably die at other ages as well.

Wedger: Of course, but it's called the 27 Club.
It keeps happening. We've got to look at patterns and when you investigate, you look at a pattern. You think, why?

Cooper: Kurt Cobain. He was 27…

Wedger: Jim Morrison.

Cooper: Yeah, Hendricks.

Wedger: Loads of them. You get the same things that keep cropping up and you've got to look at these patterns.

Cooper: The numbers are key, aren't they?

Wedger: Yeah, and they allude to it. You've just got to look at the last music thing with Madonna and Sam Smith then. And again, the transgenderism.

Cooper: It's in your face, yeah.

Wedger: That's androgyny; Baphomet - the God of androgyny.

Cooper: And what we are seeing with all the trans stuff…

Wedger: We are seeing it. And again, sodomy is a big thing. The same pattern keeps coming up.

Cooper: But why though? Why the sodomy? What's the significance of that?

Wedger: Because it's an inversion of natural sex. Everything is an inversion and it's to sully and to dirty and it's to ruin what is nice. The birth rate is plummeting. It's anti-children. It's against children. This is making them non-existent.

Cooper: And they're getting them younger and younger.

Wedger: And the birth rate's falling. So, it's anti what God wants - it's against creation.

And it's quite straightforward and I think now's the time to pick a side and see these patterns in society.

Cooper: It's what we spoke about, to get these kids very early on to corrupt them and to capture them mentally so you've got them as mind control victims. And then they are disseminated into different fields of work and they reach the top, so they're used as puppets? Is that right?

Wedger: Yeah. This guy told me that again, there's something I can go into, this thing called The Hunting Games and stuff like this.

This guy was used. They would get tramps off the street and take them to a venue which crops up all the time. And again, I can back this up with what happened with this venue because it did get in the press recently. It's in New Hampshire usually. They get tramps and his job was to hunt them down, shoot them, and kill them. And he said he could strip down a Kalashnikov by the time he was like 13 he said, "I'm a super soldier".

Some are used for prostitution, so they'd use kids for prostitution. They'll be used to be taken to venues to lure people in and to compromise them and it's a very James Bond-like.

Cooper: They say they become like double agents.

Wedger: Yeah. I mean we've got to look at James Bond, 007. Well, that was a code word for John D who was the occultic advisor to Queen Elizabeth. His name was 007.

Cooper: Wow.

Wedger: He used to sign every letter "007 John D". He was an occultic, the guy that would advise the Queen, Queen Elizabeth the 1st. John D and that's where they get it from, the spy thing.

It's very interesting and again when you look at Ian Fleming, who wrote the James Bond things, who was his cousin? Christopher Lee. The man in all the horror films. From the House of Horror.

Cooper: All connected.

Wedger: It's incredible when you look back at the connections through it all. I mean, I would like if we want to carry on at another later date, I can bring artwork of people who survived this trauma and show you this artwork. All the same. All the same. It actually shows the horrors.

Cooper: The rituals and stuff?

Wedger: Yeah, again, we've got to be careful because people do get worried and frightened because those who did it are still alive and it's still ongoing. But another woman who is an award-winning artist has given permission to use her artwork.

Her artwork is so accurate that we even located a venue and I'd like to explain this venue, we went there and it was almost like a picture, a photograph of what went on.

And again, the problem is they had this altered state. So, when the information is coming out they're triggered and these different characters come out and they're all child characters because it all happens when they're children. So, they could've been electrocuted, for example. So, there'll be a character that can deal with electricity, or drowning's a big one and these characters are formulated in the mind to protect the individual from all this torture and everything else.

There are lots of people and it doesn't really get the emphasis it does. There are a lot of people suffering from this and they are traumatised not to speak and they can't. This one girl, when she comes to talk, you can actually see her struggling to speak.

Cooper: These are like the "intergenerationals" would we say? Because they're kept alive, whereas the ones that aren't part of that generation, they're killed.

Wedger: Yeah, they're killed.

Cooper: And so, they're then used for prostitution, passed around maybe within those groups. And then also well, a multitude of things, right?

Wedger: Yeah. You can see it with some celebrities. I mean look at Britney Spears when she flipped and had that bizarre moment. She kept going into different personalities.

Now again, I'm not saying this person's involved in that, I'm not but there's a Come Dine With Me (TV Show) with Michael Barrymore.

Cooper: He's on the RAINS list, by the way.

Wedger: He's on the RAINS list, he's named on there. Now again, this is my opinion here. Watch it and you see different characters. His character changes on it. Even his voice changes. Actually, in one of them, he's speaking with a different voice. It is really freaky.

I think he goes to Pat Sharp's house and starts smashing plates and he's being a buffoon and an absolute weirdo, he's actually talking totally different, he's a totally different character. And he's not even jesting. It's really weird. And I'm thinking who knows? You just don't know.

Look, I've interviewed many sex offenders, paedophiles, and child abusers. How many do you think, when I asked them, "did you rape the child?" How many went, "oh yeah, I did that and I did many more".

Well, do you know they all sort of said no. So, for people to lie, it's not uncommon.

If we take sinning, lying really is at the bottom rung. The murder of a child is up higher and when people say well, they don't say they did this or they denied it. Well, of course, they denied it. Are you stupid? People aren't ready to hear these things.

They don't want to hear it. And they won't. They will go into cognitive dissonance. Even when the facts are put in their face.

Cooper: They just don't want to know, do they?

Wedger: The best thing that ever happened was Jimmy Savile. Jimmy Savile was without a doubt the best thing that ever happened and it sounds perverted. Without him being exposed, I would never be a whistle blower because it was only when Jimmy Savile was exposed, whistle blowers came forward, coppers came forward. A couple of them, brave ones, not the most of them.

Cooper: Not many, no.

Wedger: Most of them sold their soul and said nothing. Shame on them, which is most of them. But a couple of good ones did come forward as a result of Jimmy Savile and it got out. It was because of that, I was thinking, I'm not alone.

Cooper: But we've now kicked on a few years since then and there are going to be some celebrities who are still heavily involved that were protected by higher people, protected by the news, papers, the media etc. Why, if we've moved on so much, why are they not being named? Because he won't be the one high profile name.

Wedger: Yeah. For one thing, it's called picking low-hanging fruit. They'll drop the idiots. They'll get it. They'll give you one every now and then.

Cooper: Throw you a bone every now and then.

Wedger: Yeah. There's a trial going through the Scottish courts from satanism at the moment. There are 11 defendants in the Strathclyde area in Glasgow.

I actually got contacted by a family member, one of them, saying their brother was stitched up. I'm not interested, I'm not even going there.

But again, they're all junkies. It's low level. It's not the real stuff and that's what it would be, the dysfunctional council house idiots that get caught up in a little bit of witchcraft or something like that, where animals are killed.

They'll never give us the real stuff, they will never. It won't happen. And certain newspapers always crop up to denigrate those, all the time. All the time you see the same ones. I've been attacked by one satirical magazine and again, lo and behold, the editor of that is on the RAINS list!

The one thing is, if you upset a satanist, you're doing a good job. As far as I'm concerned, I'm not here for them. I'm here to do what I do. But just watch the space, it will come out.

Cooper: Is it coming out? Do you reckon it's all coming out?

Wedger: Yeah, it will. Things like this will encourage it to come out. Be careful because there are a lot of damaged people. One minute they will love you, one minute, they will hate you and you get the most vexed trolling when you speak out against satanism. Awful, appalling, nasty, horrible but I don't care, they don't bother me. They don't interest me. I've not got nothing to hide from these people.

Even in the height of my whistle blowing, I wrote to Cressida Dick and I told her, don't ever go and get a warrant. I will always let you in my house. I will always make my door available for you. I'll even send you a key. You don't need a warrant, you can come to my house anytime and search it and any data storage device or phone, whatever you want, I will surrender it. Whatever you want. I've got nothing to hide. Absolutely nothing to hide. If you find something at my house then it's a bonus.

It's rare, I even have alcohol in my house. There's nothing they have that I want. And I'm here to do what I do. I want to expose this. I want it to keep coming out. I implore survivors to come out and be strong.

Whenever a war is waged, they have to denigrate the enemy. They have to give them… like the Nazis, they called them Jerry's. They always have to denigrate because then they're not human. And then you can kill them and you can offer them up. Do you know what I mean?

So, whenever a victim comes out, they have to denigrate them; they're a "junkie", they're a "liar", they're "nuts", they're "schizophrenic", they're this, they're that.

But I'll say, just stand up and keep going. Do not be frightened of these people. You owe them absolutely nothing. They're the cowards because they rape children.

They're perverts and cowards and if they weren't, then tell the world what you do but they won't do it because they're frightened.

Do not be frightened of them. They're rotting in hell anyway. They might as well make the most of their life because the moment they shut their eyes, and draw their last breath, they are truly royally fucked.

Now, I'm not saying I know what's on the other side, but I have a good belief that I know. If I'm wrong, so what? What's the problem?

What if I'm right?

What if I'm right, that there is judgment, and this is against God and you're going to rot? If I'm right, they are fucked and everyone who aligns himself with Satan, they are screwed too.

I call out to satanists, stop it. Stop it. I call out to the paedophiles, stop it. Stop doing it. Repent what you do. Cause no more pain, stop this time. There is time. Go to Jesus, repent, turn it in, don't do it anymore.

I say to all those that are suffering, suicide is not the answer. Please, do not do suicide. It's not the answer. There is another way.

There's a thing I'm doing I'd like to say it's called #PSAD. I should have worn a T-shirt. Pants Swimming Against Depression. I've been going all around the UK throughout the coldest days of the winter in my underpants swimming in rivers, lakes, canals, and reservoirs in my pants, I've been doing it. I've done it in the snow, the ice, and the rain, as cold-water therapy. It really does work, (only if you can swim obviously otherwise you're in trouble!) But it does and I just want to really re-masculate the men and it's mainly aimed at men, but cold-water therapy works. It genuinely works. Suicide is not the answer. It really isn't.

Whoever did these things to you, it's them that are at fault, not you. Do not harbour that guilt. Do not hang on to that guilt. Get rid of that, it's not your guilt. You never did that, they did that to you. You had no choice. They were an adult, you weren't. They had a choice, you didn't. Shame on them. Don't carry that shame, give it up.

Each time you go through life with all that on your back, every year it's another rock in there and it will soon weigh you down. Get rid of it. It aint your pain. Give it up and speak out. Speak out. And if the police don't take it on, complain, set up a working group. Keep going.

Cooper: I was going to say, is it possible that we could draft up a letter that people can also use to put pressure on their MP's or something like that? That might be useful.

Wedger: You can do it. I've done it before. I've set up campaign letters for Cressida Dick.

I set it up against this officer that's on the RAINS list that's named; the ex-vice officer, saying that he shouldn't be having his pension, that he should be arrested and held accountable for his involvements against children. Nothing was ever done.

Cooper: Yeah, but if we get enough people who are watching this video [or reading this book] they can all send the same sort of letter, know how to write it, know what to say. Is that worth it, is that something worth doing?

Wedger: Yeah. I think it may be, yeah. Find an MP or whatever that will listen or even send it to the Home Secretary.

What would be good is that the Home Office recognises SRA and it's an aggravating factor to child murder and to child sexual abuse. That it is an add-on.

You could punch someone in the face, that's ABH, right? Punch someone in the face *and* call them a "bender" or something like that... that's a "homophobic assault". Or call them, I don't know, an ethnically derogatory name, that's "racially aggravated". Well, why can't we have it as a faith-based thing on this?

So, if the satanists say what they have is a religion, well then become faith-based, and then let's take you to court for crimes against children and crimes against humanity. And let's hope the police enforce it.

But this is how it works and open your doors to what goes on, like all the other faiths have to but they won't, they won't. It won't happen. But that would be a lovely thing to achieve.

Again, in my journey, I've interviewed Exorcists from the Roman Catholic Church and interviewed one in Luton - the top Exorcist in the UK. A lovely guy. He is retired now. Beautiful man.

There's a film called Deliver us from Evil about a Vatican Exorcist which was Malachi Martin and an NYPD copper which is a guy I know called Ralph Sachi, Detective Ralph Sachi, and Ralph Sachi is a lovely man and these two teamed up. Officially teamed up.

It was sanctioned by the NYPD and they were to go to suspicious homicides which had a ritualistic twist to them and they were investigated as satanic ritual abuse cases and they were highly successful and they would interview survivors of it and Malachi Martin would come in and they would do exorcisms and all that. They had psychiatrists working with them.

It was funded by the Catholic Church in Ireland, they paid for it but they recognised it and they went on to prosecute many people and that's the NYPD. Deliver us from Evil - it's out there. It's a really good film and it's true, it's true.

Ralph, I think the last few years he's retired. I was in close contact with him. We all network in this world. We do know each other.

The satanists all know me, *all* know me. I've had dead animals left outside my house. I have had talons, I've had trackers put on my car, I've had wreaths put out, I had a wreath put out the back of my house once.

All these out there were bizarre and like dolls made out of grass and things like that laid out somewhere and I was just about to do a charity walk and I felt for about five days, like I'd been stabbed. I was in so much pain. It was like I'd been stabbed.

I had this big chicken talon was placed outside. Oh, it was weird. Dead birds and all sorts of things.

Cooper: Has the prayer worked then? Do you think it helped?

Wedger: Yeah, 100%. I know a group from the travelling community that speak out about ritualistic stuff and they've had very similar stuff done to them as well.

It does work but don't give it the power. God's got your back, He's got your back on this. Give it back to them, return it to the sender. Let no weapon formed against me prosper. Send it back to them and I just say speak out. Speak out. And if I want to leave it in the words of Edmund Burke, "the only thing necessary for the triumph of evil is for good men to do nothing", and that's all it takes, simple as that.

Well, let's not be in a game of doing nothing. Let's do something.

Speak out. Find your voice. You don't need to be Mr Universe, a tough guy and all that to do this. Your own resolve can do it.

Cooper: A bit of courage.

Wedger: A bit of courage is all it takes. These are cowards.
We're up against cowards and that's what they are, people who prey on children. They're not men (and women). They're not human beings. These are nothing. They shouldn't do it and we shouldn't let it either.

Also, I want to finish by talking about the root cause to most of this. Kids are coming from abuse at home. Now we can blame the police and we can blame the social services all we want but you know… and this upsets people what I say… but where's the lioness when the cubs are hurt?

Men… where are the men exactly? Where are the men? Don't punch your chest out and stand there being the big guy, when you've walked out on your own children. That don't wash.

Your job is to protect your children. Not your car, not your trainers, your *children.* We are failing our children on a masculine front - *men.*

So what has happened to the British men? Where have they gone? Where are the warriors we once had? It's appalling.

Single parenting. This baby mother/baby father culture that has been pushed on us. It's been patronised by the music industry, by popular culture, by TV and it has, all for the fear of insulting people.

You know what, I don't care if I insult an adult, I really don't and you would have gathered that from some of the backlash you get with trolling when anyone has me on, I don't care.

My job is to protect children, not to placate adults. It isn't you know. If I had my own way, children would all be born in marriage. I was a single parent, I had children outside of marriage, I ended up bringing up children on my own. Not just mine but other people's children. I lived in poverty. I am qualified to make these assumptions, these accusations and take this quite staunch standpoint on this because you know it's our children that suffer. It's not the adults, it's the children that suffer.

The social services system needs to change. Children should not be treated as a commodity. When people take on fostering, they should not be allowed respite care. Why should you be allowed to go on holiday and then the kid goes off out into a kennel somewhere like some dog. You invite a kid into a household, you love it and you care for it, like it's your own. It should not be a business. People are running it as businesses now.

There is so much corruption in local government regarding fostering it's untrue. It needs government regulation and it needs absolute scrutiny and then there is also this dogged attack on families to try and find dysfunctionality to break them up because the kids make a lot of money.

But when people say to me, "what do I do, I've got social services on my case"?

I said, "you keep your house clean, keep it tidy, make sure there's food in the cupboard. If you've got a dog, walk it. Don't have dog shit in your house. Especially with a kid in there. Keep your own house in order. You can go to Poundland and buy a bottle of bleach, it's a quid, it'll kill it, it'll sterilise everything, so when they come round, you're not giving the social workers ammunition".

And enjoy spending your time with your children, go for a walk, it's free! They say, the best things in life are free and they are. It's just no one wants to put in hard work anymore, they don't. We've become lazy, we've become slobs. You've got women with no ability to cook, no idea of nutrition. This should be instilled at school but again, it's not politically correct to do so. There's been a deliberate erosion of what is good and what isn't good and people have lost their way spiritually.

Cooper: Funny you should say, I was in Brighton and I saw a mum giving her little baby Coca-Cola and I said, "what are you doing? You're gonna kill that baby". And she looked at me like I was some nutter.

Wedger: Not only that, if you go out here, you'll see a row of shops and you'll have a chicken shop, a pizza shop, then this shop, then that kebab shop, all selling crap.

We've had this huge influx of Eastern Europeans that have got still got very staunch family values - they cook, their children sit and eat at the table, they're answerable to their parents.

So men, protect your children. Mothers, be good mothers. And people, look out for your community. Do what they do in tribal areas. Look out for each other. Protect your children. Protect them and nurture them. It will pay back someday. Don't let anyone hurt them.

Cooper: And yes, protect your community. All the stuff going on at the moment, with the grooming of children sexually, and politically. We need the strong men to push back on some of this stuff that we are seeing.

Wedger: Yeah, and unfortunately, there are a lot of young men that have got nowhere to turn to. They are after role models. And that's because there's no real father figure in their communities anymore. And we need to bring that back. We need to.

And love your children because they're not here for long. They're not. In the blink of an eye, they're grown up. Let's make them grow up into solid, strong, nice human beings and we'll see society change, we will.

Cooper: I think it's such an important message that I just feel like this is where I'm gravitating towards with my work.

Wedger: I think it's great what you've got going here. Look, years ago, the podcast would be like a 10-minute thing. Now, people listen to go to the gym and listen everywhere to it.

It's like the radio, they'll sit and they'll do a day's work and so they go on for an hour or two hours. Some can be a bit laborious but others you're riveted to them.

This can go on and it's a fascinating subject. The depths we can go to with this is incredible and then you can pass it on to survivors and get them to give their testimonies.

But my approach… and I know it might not be that of the show but my approach is for Jesus Christ and that's because life took me that way. I've seen a miracle with my son and I've seen evil and I have faced evil and maybe another time, I'll tell you about that and I've encountered it, a truly possessed individual and it's horrible and it's frightening. So, I'm blessed. Thank you so much.

Cooper: Thank you so much. Thanks to Jon again for sharing his time with us and his story and still standing in that courage and standing in that truth. As part of this podcast, we're trying to courageously bring all this out into the light. So long may that continue.

All right everyone, this is Raising the Bar with myself John Cooper. Thank you.

Final Note

Thank you for taking the time to read The Great Reveal. Please help support this message by sharing this book with your friends and family. Additionally, your reviews on Amazon are really important to help the book gain visibility, reaching more potential readers.

For those who wish to explore further, I invite you to join me on my podcast Raising the Bar. In this podcast, we delve into a range of topics including psychology, philosophy, science, and current affairs. It is a platform built on raw, honest journalism, presenting thought-provoking interviews and discussions that aim to be a beacon of light in a sea of mainstream media lies and deception.

Together, let us stand against darkness and champion the pursuit of truth.

Thank you.

John Cooper

youtube.com/thejohncoopershow

Printed in Great Britain
by Amazon

42777691R00126